# MADOL DOOVA
# මඩොල් දුව

## WRITINGS BY MARTIN
## WICKRAMASINGHE IN ENGLISH

Aspects of Sinhalese Culture
Buddhist Jataka Stories and the Russian Novel
Mysticism of Lawrence
Buddhism and Culture
Buddhism and Art
Revolution and Evolution
Sinhala Language and Culture

### _Translations in English_
Landmarks of Sinhala Literature
Madol Doova
Lay Bare the Roots  (අපේ ගම)
The Way of the Lotus (විරාගය)
Selected Short Stories  (තෝරාගත් කෙටි කතා)
Uprooted - The Village  - (ගම්පෙරළිය)
_The English Translation of Gamperaliya_

# Martin Wickramasinghe's

# MADOL DOOVA

# මඩොල් දූව

Translated
by
ASHLEY HALPE

SARASA (PVT) LIMITED
18/3, Kirimandala Mawatha
NAWALA, RAJAGIRIYA
SRI LANKA
Tel: 011-2865543, 5373621  Fax: 011-2866938

# Martin Wickramasinghe's
# Madol Doova

| | |
|---|---|
| First Published (Sinhala) | 1947 |
| 58th Sinhala Edition | 2012 |

### Translations:

| | |
|---|---|
| Russian | 1954 |
| Rumanian | 1962 |
| Chinese | 1961 |
| Bulgarian | 1964 |
| English | 1976 |
| Dutch | 1979 |
| Tamil | 1997 |
| Japanese | 2002 |
| Italian | 2009 |

Thirtieth English Edition          2012

*Copyright reserved*

The copyright of this book belong to the Martin Wickramasinghe Trust. This book should not be reprinted, published, distributed or sold, either in part or in its entirety without the permission of the Martin Wickramasinghe Trust.

**ISBN 956-8415-09-X**

Printed by
**K.S.U. GRAPHIC (PVT) LTD**
510, Rajagiriya Road
Rajagiriya.
Sri Lanka
Tel: 011-2884701 Fax: 011-2882323
E-mail: ksugraphic@yahoo.com

# CONTENTS

# LICENCE
## MINISTRY OF EDUCATION

**Name of the book :-** Madol Doova

**Author :-** Martin Wickramasinghe

<u>Licence</u>

My No: EPAB2/ 8488

Approved as a School Library book by the Director General of Education in terms of para 19/A of the Code of Regulations for Assisted Vernecular, Bilingual and English Schools published in the Government Gazette of 29th February, 1952.

Vijitha Welagedara
Secretary
Educational Publications
Advisory Board.

2009.12.21
Ministry of Education & Higher Education
'Isurupaya' Battaramulla

## Martin Wickramasinghe website:
## www.martinwickramasinghe.info

The Website is maintained by
**THE MARTIN WICKRAMASINGHE TRUST**
18/3, Kirimandala Mawatha, Nawala, Rajagiriya, Sri Lanka.
Tel : 011- 2865543 - 5373621 Fax : 011-2866938,
E-mail : mwtrust@lankabellnet.com.

# MADOL DOOVA

## NOTE TO THE ENGLISH TRANSLATION

*Madol Doova* is rich in blithe escapades of rural boyhood. The spirit of youthful mischief comes vividly to life in such episodes as the cadju raid, the Veddah game or the dish of live frogs. Grown-up opposition only add spice to the narrative, while there is a delightful account of the exploits of a confidence trickster. Viewed in this light, *Madol Doova* is a sequence of lively, neatly shaped episodes with a plausible and very human connecting story, the hunt for the floating flame forming the climax of what might be called the adventures of Upali Giniwelle and his follower Jinna.

Yet *Madol Doova* ends soberly, even somberly. The story begins too, with Upali recalling his mother's death and the consequent changes in the pattern of his relationships. The adventure element and the scenes of mischief are placed in a realistic context: the lifeblood of *Madol Doova,* one might say, is the detail of life in the rural-south, half a century ago. Persons, places and the vicissitudes of daily life are given fullness and warm immediacy, while in every episode there is a deft balance of the unusual and the typical.

It is in relation to these realities that the connecting tale gains an added dimension of humane relevance, A taste for our out-door life, a love of independence and even sheer boyish venturesomeness lead Upali and Jinna away from the accustomed paths of the rural middle class. They strike out for themselves. In doing so, and without conscious choice, they meet reality on their own terms. They stake out anew life on

Madol Doova showing a resourcefulness and staying power that had earlier found no acceptable outlet. At the time the novel was written the idea of a boy hero fending for himself as a small farmer might have seemed a fictional extravagance: today, it seems almost prophetic. At the end of the novel we find Upali capable of caring for his stepmother and her son when his father dies. He has not turned his back on Madol Dova rather, Madol Doova has brought him to the threshold of maturity.

Martin Wickramasinghe maintains a lightness of touch from beginning to end. There is no trace of sententiousness and there is always the sense of reading a lively story. Within this framework, the experience of boyhood are enriched by the perceptions of the mature artist.

A.H.

# CHAPTER I

# ROBBERS

Mother died when I was about seven years old. At least, that is what I have heard father and my stepmother say. I can still remember how father and my aunt the other relatives wept at the funeral. I cried because everyone else was doing so. When my aunt carried me out into the garden, a woman stroked my head and kissed me, and said "Aney! The poor motherless thing!"

One day, some time later, father brought my stepmother and a crowd of relatives to the house in a fleet of horse-carriages. I remember very clearly how father climbed down from the carriage with my stepmother and came up to the verandah. She kept her eyes on the ground and father walked so close to her that their bodies almost touched. It was much later that I learnt from the gossiping of the women that father married a second time about a year after mother died.

I soon realized that my stepmother was not like mother. She didn't care for me in the same way, even though she was much more loving and attentive to father than my mother had been. The women sometimes told me that she was a miser, but I didn't understand what they meant until I was little older.

She was very careful with the housekeeping money that father gave her. She scolded the servants all the time and even quarreled with them. "You are wasting the sugar!" she shouted, if the tea was too sweet. She always went to the kitchen after every meal to give out the servant's food herself. If the rice and curry wasn't enough they had to ask her for a second helping. She managed to save some of the housekeeping money and went into pawn-broking with it. She charged five cents a month on a rupee an interest of sixty percent.

Father was very pleased when he heard about this for he worked very hard at his shop. He gave her a hundred rupees to help her with her business.

About a year later my stepmother had a son. When my brother was about three years old and I was about eleven I began to feel a difference in her treatment of us. She wasn't unkind to me, even though she didn't love me as mother has done. But I saw how much she loved her own son and it made me jealous and unhappy. That's really why I turned against her. She too, began to change about the same time. I am not sure whether it was because my brother was growing older or because I had already begun to treat her differently. I don't think it was her fault, but I began to get into trouble more and more often. Perhaps it would have been different if mother had lived. Perhaps it was also because I had more of my father in me. He never listened to anyone.

I didn't like studying and going to school. I wanted to be out all the time, playing with my friends wrestling or fighting with them or going swimming in the sea or in the river. I even fought with boys who were much bigger than I. Sometimes I returned home with a bruised face or bleeding arm.Sometimes the mother of a boy whom I had hurt came home to complain about me to father. This made father very angry and he gave me a beating.

My stepmother began to complain about me to father more and more often. I don't know whether she liked seeing me beaten. But I wasn't a boy who could be kept down by beating.

When my stepmother made a special sweet or a delicacy she always put father's share aside first before giving me any. I usually took my share to the kitchen to give the servants a bit, too. On days when father didn't come home at noon I ate in the kitchen, sitting on a rickety old chair. I did this because I felt so sorry about the way the sevants were constantly scolded by my stepmother.

The boy who worked for us was actually a poor relation, the son of a distant aunt of father's. He was about three years older than I. His name was Jinapala but I usually called him "Jine" or "Jinna". He did hardly any work about the house, for he was always joining in my games or playing truant. I would find him waiting for me by the roadside when I came out of school.

Halfway between our house and the school was a deserted *ambalama*. It stood on a piece of land surrounded by a low wall. We used to steal the young coconuts from the four trees that grew there. Jinna climbed the trees and threw down the nuts and I divided them among the boys.

As soon as I got back from school I would throw my books and slate on the table or on my bed and rush away to play with my friends. Jinna followed me. This was what he waited for all day. My stepmother scolded him and even beat him but she couldn't keep him back.

We usually went to a sandy stretch near a small wood not far from the village. To the right of the wood was a spring well, to which people from the village came all morning to bathe. In the evening the poor women and the servants from the rich families came for water. They stayed a while, laughing and gossiping before they went back to the village in groups with their pots on their hips. Young men from the village often came there in the evenings to look at the girls and to get a chance of talking to them or chatting with them.

The thickets gave us shelter. The leaves grew so thickly overhead that we only had to run in under the trees when it rained to be completely sheltered. One thicket was as good as a tent even in the heaviest downpour and this was our special hiding place.

On Saturdays and Sundays we played, ran and wrestled on the sand all day. When the scorching sun was too much for us our thicket sheltered us better than any hut we could have built for ourselves. We had made a platform of sticks on which two could lie at a time.

One day we were all trying to think of something new to play.

I've had enough of *katti* said Jinna. "We play it every day!"

"And I'm sick of wrestling" said Siripala.

"Right, then let's be robbers today", I said.

The others clapped their hands at this. "How do we become robbers?" asked Ranadeva.

"Just wait a bit, will you?"

I told them what we could do.

"I'm going to be the chief."

They applauded.

Everyone must do as I say, or it'll be the worse for you. The chief is horribly cruel right? No one, is to break the rules. You'll be sorry if you do. Do you hear? No one is to tell anybody our names, whatever happens. Do you know how traitors will be punished? We'll kill you! Right."

That frightened, and they looked cautiously at each other all except Jinna.

"That's too much, let's leave our killing" said Siripala.

"No! That's no way for a gang of robbers to talk.

You know what they did in the old days? Traitors were hacked in two and the pieces strung up on a tree."

That settled Siripala.

"All right, Jinna will be the house breaker today.

The house breaker must only wear a black loin cloth. Do you hear? In the old days a house breaker used to oil himself all over, make himself slippery, see? If people in the house woke up and tried to catch him he could just slip out of their grasp. And we must all tie black cloth over our eyes."

"What's that for? How could we see anything then? Asked Dangadasa.

"You make two big holes for your eyes. One robber breaks into the house. The chief and all others keep watch. If anyone comes, we tie him up. If he tries to fight, I'll cut him down with my sword!" I pulled out my sword and sliced off the top of a kidaram bush with one blow. The others looked at me in awe. My sword was only a hoop from a barrel which I had beaten flat and fitted up with a wooden handle.

"As soon as you get into the house you break open the *almariya* .....see? Get the jewellery and the money and clear out....Fast" I ordered. "If anybody wakes up before we get away and comes after us we knock him down. But don't hurt the children whatever happens. You have heard of Ali Baba and the Forty Thieves, haven't you?"

"Yes"

"Well, we will disguise ourselves like the forty thieves and go to Babun *Mudalali's* house. We'll get in by asking for shelter and then rob him. But that'll have to wait. We must get some practice before we try a thing like that."

I pulled off the black handkerchief I used as a belt and cut holes in it for a mask. I did the same with a piece from Jinna's sarong. The others didn't want to tear their sarongs.

"My mother will beat me," said Dnagadasa.

"So what? Afraid? That won't do. Robbers mustn't be scared of anybody!"

But they ran back to their homes to fetch strips of black cloth.

"Siripala, wait! Bring some coconut oil with you about a quarter bottle."

"Coconut oil? What for?"

"To rub on Jinna's body."

Siripala was soon back with the oil and a piece of black cloth torn from his grandfather's old umbrella. Dangadasa had found a tattered red handkerchief and a ragged piece of a brown sarong. Jinna tore off a strip of this for his loin cloth. I rubbed the coconut oil all over his body and tied his piece of black cloth tightly over his eyes.

"Can you see all right?"

"Yes, Yes, I can see, my eyes aren't covered."

The others too, tied on their masks

"Oho! Where are the housebreaking tools?" I asked. They looked about vaguely. Dangadasa scratched his head thoughtfully.

"There's a small crowbar at home," he said.

"That's fine, fetch it quick! Bring an old *kaththa* too, if you can.".

Dangadasa returned with the tools. I tied on my black handkerchief and flourished my sword. We set off.

"Wait a minute," I said. "Siripala, you're the scout today. Go on ahead and see if there's anyone at the watchman's house. Be quick, now!"

The watchman's house was about a quarter of a mile away, on the other side of our wood.

"Only an old woman and two children," reported Siripala.

"Fine. That's just the thing for our first job! We can't take on a house where there are grown up men yet. We'll do that next time. Let's go!"

There was no window in the back wall of the watchman's house. I ordered Jinna to make a hole in the wall. The three others and I kept watch from different places around the house.

"Idiot! Why are you digging into the foundation?" I asked. "You'll end up under the floor. Make a hole just above the ground."

"My lord! The wall is made of wattle and mud. If I go higher we'll have to cut through bamboo and *eramudu*."

I signaled to Dangadasa.

"Run to the carpenter's. Steal a saw from the shed. No one must see you!"

"It's easy," said Siripala. "Uparis is deaf he can't hear at all unless you shout in his ear. He must be resting on his bed in the verandah now and the shed is behind the house. You'll get in easily."

Dangadasa didn't take long. Jinna knocked away chunks of mud and then began to cut through the strips of bamboo with the saw.

The old woman heard the rasping noise and went round to the back of the house. At first our masks scared her, but then she saw what Jinna was doing. 'Apoi'!" She shouted and ran at him.

"Stop!" I yelled, jumping between them, and pointing my sword at her. She stopped dead. She looked terrified.

"We're robbers!"

But the sight of Jinna sawing away at the wattles was too much for her.

"*Mala Ilawwa!* You'll bring down the house! They have been given too much to eat, that's what! Stop it!" She picked up a stick and went for Jinna. I dropped my sword and grabbed her by the waist. The other three ran to us, tripped her and held her down. She tried to scream for help. I got my sword and held it over her.

"Don't you open your mouth, if you value your life! We are robbers!"

I fetched a creeper and tied her hands up tightly.

"Sons of she-devils! Shameless bastards! They eat so much they can't keep quiet! Let me go, you filthy dogs! They must have eaten the holy offerings!......"

"Hey, you watch out or else.....we're robbers! Said Dangadasa, trying to imitate me.

"You rascals! I don't care what you are! Let me go!" She screamed again.

The two children crept out of the house and peeped round the wall. When they saw our masked faces they screamed and ran away. Men and women rushed out of the houses nearby.

"Jinna, stop! People are coming!" Jinna got up, the saw and the crowbar still in his hands.

"Run! All of you!"

When they had got away, I looked back. Some of the women saw me and came after me. I ran into a thicket. They untied the old woman. I could still hear her scolding us angrily.

When I'd got safely into the wood I scouted round quietly for a bit. Then I pulled my whistle from my belt and blew it. The others came creeping up to where I was.

"They'll come after us. No running away, now! We'll fight! If one man comes after us we just tie him up, if it's two we knock down one and tie up the other, see? Then we get away."

Jinna immediately stood guard, holding out his crowbar threateningly. Dangadasa waved his *kattha* in the air, the others grabbed two big sticks. Then we crept through the wood to our usual hiding place and sat on the platform keeping a good look out for pursuers.

## CHAPTER II

# THE VEDDAH GAME

The whole village was agog next day because no one had been able to recognize the boys who had broken into the watchman's house.

"It must have been a gang of boys from another village," some people said.

"But the watchman's mother said that two of them looked like Upali and Dangadasa," said one woman. Upali Giniwelle- that's my name."

Nobody said anything about Jinna. Our parents didn't punish us because they didn't know for sure whether we were the boys. It was a good thing that they did not think of looking at the black handkerchief round my waist!"

"How did you tear that sarong?" My stepmother asked Jinna.

"Oh, it got caught in the fence," he said.

She didn't believe him of course, but there was nothing to connect him with the gang.

But our parents began to keep an eye on us. My stepmother was watching me all the time. For nearly a week we played nothing but *Kalli*, *Pandu* and *Katti*.

About two weeks passed. People forgot about the housebreaking. The watchman no longer threatened us, his mother stopped scolding us whenever she saw us. We began to play in the woods again.

Sometimes we hid in the bushes by the path through the woods and shot at passing villagers with our catapults. Now and then we managed to hit someone on the ankle. "Oo!" He'd cry, rubbing his ankle and peering into the bushes. But no one spotted us. They went on their way abusing all boys in general. If they had caught sight of us they would have complained to our parents at once.

One Sunday evening we were playing in the woods, when someone suggested playing *Veddahs*. We rolled up our sarongs and tied them up like loin cloths. We strung *burulla* leaves together and draped them round our waists and made ourselves headgear of *kos*-leaf. I even had a big strong bow with arrows of pointed bamboo. The others had smaller bows and their arrows were mere *iratu*.

I slung the bow over my left shoulder and the others followed suit. We started out, peering into the undergrowth, a band of *Veddahs* on the alert for beast or foe.

We soon came to the further part of the wood, near the spring well to which everyone came for water. Three girls were at the well chatting and laughing and we crouched in the thicket watching them. One of the girls pushed another and burst out laughing. The third caught her round the waist and kissed her in the face. Then the first girl looked around cautiously and began to dance while her friends laughed and clapped their hands.

"If anyone sees us we'll be hunted out of the village," said the girl who was dancing.

"Look! This is how the *Opisera-Hamine* walks." One of them imitated the wife of the village headman.

"Ah! But that's nothing! You should see how *Subehamy Mudalali's* wife struts along," said another. She was talking about my stepmother. The other two egged her on to imitate my stepmother's walk.

"*Inda*! The silly old coquette!"

We couldn't help laughing quietly to ourselves. One of the girls went to the stone slab beside the well. She tied a rope round the neck of her pot and lowered it in. I know that they would go back to the village as soon as they had filled their pots.

"Look, the does are drinking from the pond!" I said unslinging my bow.

"Shall we shoot?" said Ranadeva.

I took aim at one of the girls and let fly. "*Apoi*, amme!" she cried out and slipped down to the ground holding on to the side of the well. My friends shot four more arrows. Two fell into the water, two hit a girl and fell on to the slab.

"We got one!" we shouted and rushed out of our thicket. Two of the girls ran away with their pots. The injured girl held her bleeding leg and moaned.

We lifted her and carried her into the thicket. She began to shriek but no one seemed to hear.

"Shut up, you!" I threatened her, "We're *Veddahs*!"

"Please, I only mimicked your stepmother for a joke!" She pleaded. She was quite frightened and began to cry.

"We've made a mistake," I said, "We were after deer, but we've shot a woman. We mistook these girls for does!"

"What shall we do now?" asked Ranadeva.

"We'll have to get something for the wound. And if she can't walk, we'll have to carry her back."

"Does? You shot at does?" She looked around.

"I can walk. Really! Please don't carry me again!'

"Come on!" I called to the others. I tore a strip off Jinna's sarong. Ranadeva bent down to move her cloth away from the wound.

"*Apoi*!" she screamed and knocked his hand away. She crouched away from us, holding down her cloth.

"Shut up, you!" I threatened her with the bow. Ranadeva and Siripala got hold of her hands while Dangadasa held her down by her hips. She struggled and then began to giggle as if we were tickling her.

I knelt and lifted the corner of her cloth and cleaned the bleeding wound near her knee. We crushed some leaves into a pad and put it on the wound. We bandaged her leg with the strip of cloth.

She seemed to be enjoying the game now.

"She can't walk yet," I said to the other *Veddahs*.

"We'll have to carry her!"

"*Apoi*! Please don't people might see. I can walk now," she said.

"Quiet!" I said fiercely. "What do we care about people? "We are *Veddahs*!"

Despite her struggles we carried her through the woods and put her down near the well. She lifted the pot to her hip and walked away quickly. But she kept looking back to smile at us.

Soon all sorts of tales about our hunting expedition were rife in the village.

Upali Giniwelle and four other scamps hid in the trees near the pond. They carried off Lamahewage Nadoris's youngest daughter into the jungle."

"Incredible! The smell of mother's milk is still on their lips and they do a thing like that! Some grownup must have been behind it! It could only be that Hinnimahattaya."

Hinnimahattaya was the youngest son of the village headman. He was supposed to be the village rake.

"How disgusting to make use of children for such things!"

Lalitha swore that there hadn't been anybody but us. The children had only been playing *Veddahs*. She had fallen only because she had been hit by an arrow. It hadn't hurt much but the shock had made her scream and lose her balance. She told them how we had carried her off screaming into the jungle only to put some herbs on her wound and carry her back.

"How is it that no one heard you scream?" asked one of the villagers.

"I screamed twice, but then Upali Punchimahattaya threatened me."

"Huh! threatened you?" snorted the villager. "And you let a child like that frighten you? Are you such a baby? All right. What were you doing all the time they were attending to your wound in the jungle? Why didn't you scream then? You enjoyed it didn't you? Didn't you say so yourself to the other girls?"

"Because I realized it was only a game."

This only made the women scold her more.

"We shouldn't blame those poor children. It's all her own fault! Why did she have to fall? It was only a thin sliver of bamboo, after all! Would a big girl like that faint so easily? The whole thing must be a put up job. She must have been in it from the first. We should punish her, not the children!"

"Imagine what it will be like when their shoulders reach the height their heads are now! It won't be safe for a girl to step out of the house!"

But Lalitha had the worst of it. She had to give up going to the spring well and for nearly six months she bathed at a desolate well on the other side of the village.

Father beat me mercilessly and locked me up for three days with one leg clamped into a pillory. This was how boys who did not regard a beating seriously were punished in those days.

But this didn't make me sorry for what I had done at all. My love of adventure only increased. A month later the school master came to see father and told him that I was cutting school.

"What! Upali leaves every morning and he comes home at the time you close school. Last month, of course he could not go to school for a week because I had punished him for his scandalous behaviour."

"Then he must be playing truant all day and getting home at just the right time!"

"I'll pack you off to Maggona!" father threatened me after the school master had gone. I didn't know then that Maggona was a reformatory.

I couldn't understand why father wouldn't let me play outdoors all day. I hated books and I was tired of sitting on a bench with a book in front of me. I wanted to go rowing on the river. I loved violent exercise, I thought of running away with Jinna, but he wouldn't agree.

I wished I could join the men who went digging for gems in the Ratnapura jungles. I knew that boys went with them to help in the work. I remembered the stories I had heard of desperadoes who went with exorcists into the vast forests near Anuradhapura in search of hidden treasure. There were stories about dynamiting rocks, smashing statues and killing giant cobras who were the guardians of fabulous treasure troves. If I could join a band of treasure hunters! I dreamt of escaping. I felt sure I could outdo Aladdin if only I could get away.

Father spent all day in his shop and got back late every evening. My stepmother spent her time bathing, feeding and cuddling her baby or seeing to things about the house. She didn't forget to scold me and tell me to be a good boy. The biggest thing in the lives of the women was the daily gossip at the well. The young men went to the well to make fun of the girls or to flirt with them. On full moon days everybody went to the temple and sat on the floor to listen to a sermon. It was all so dull no better than going to school.

Father must have decided that I would become a real bad character if I were to stay in the village any longer. He took me to Welikanda and left me with the headmaster of the school there. Perhaps my stepmother was in it too. I was becoming a nuisance and a menace to her and she might have thought of getting rid of me for a while.

One Sunday afternoon father and I took the bus to Welikanda. Mr.Dharmasingha Andagala, the headmaster seemed to be a great friend of my father. He welcomed us enthusiastically. He said he was happy to be of some service to father, that he hadn't forgotten how father had helped him when he was at the Kamburugamuwa school.

No one could even guess from my looks the sort of mischief I was capable of. The headmaster took to me and began to say nice things about me.

"He's a terrible scamp," said my father. "It must be our village - there's something the matter there. The children have been behaving very badly....."

"Every child is a bit of a scamp after all! There are times when my own children seem to be getting out of hand. But I don't let them go too far. I'm sure the boy will try not to get into mischief here. He will have no opportunity of making bad friends here….."

Mr.Dharmasingha spoke as if he was teaching a class, gesturing with a raised forefinger.

He looked overworked and prematurely old. His black hair was graying already. Because of this, or because he was so anaemic, he seemed pale, although he had a coal black face which made the whites of his eyes look strangely brilliant. His teeth too, seemed milk white no doubt for the same reason. He ended every sentence with "understand?" even when he was talking to father.

Mr.Dharmasingha's two children were peeping at me through the doorway. One was a boy of about eight, the other a girl, looked about six years old. I liked them, but not the schoolmaster and his wife. I wondered if Mr.Dharmasingha and his wife were thinking all the time about something they had lost, something precious, like a child. The headmaster smiled a bit when welcoming us but his face soon took on a weary and cheerless look. His wife did not seem to know how to smile or laugh. Or else she thought it sinful to smile. Perhaps that was why she glared at the children when they smiled at me.

"You must try to be a good boy," said my father when it was time for him to go. "Don't make mischief."

I went to school the next day with Mr.Dharmasingha. He put me in his own class. Only three of the boys there were bigger than I. One of them threw a  paper ball at the back of my head.

"A real *galibba*," I heard a boy say."

"A tough nut," said another.

"Silence!" thundered the headmaster, striking his desk with his cane.

## CHAPTER III

# HOW I WENT TO SEA

In two weeks all my classmates except one made friends with me. Only the boy who called me "*galibb*a" on the first day kept aloof. I liked going to school because of all my new friends, but I still hated having to study. Our books were full of tiresome old sayings and difficult words. Mr.Dharmasingha was deadly serious all the time and looked as if he was carrying some burden on his shoulders.

Somalatha and Gunadasa became quite fond of me when they saw how much I liked playing out of doors. When Mr. Dharmasingha saw that we ran out of the house to play as soon as we got home from school he began trying to interfere. "That's enough! You'd better do your home work now!" he would shout two or three times every afternoon. There were times when we stopped only when he threatened to punish us. After three or four months of this Mrs. Dharmasingha began to keep Somalatha and Gunadasa away from me. "He thinks of nothing but playing," I heard her say.

When she saw us running and jumping in the front yard she would come out to the verandah to shout "Don't run so fast, Somalatha! you'll fall!" When we played in the sand she called out "Don't kick up dust, you'll get sores all over you!" When I threw a stone at an iguana she rarely failed to shout out, "Don't be so cruel to animals, child", when we ran into the thickets nearby it was "You stay here, Somalatha, the nettles will sting you", if we went to the gate it was "Don't you go out – there are cars going down that road!" But how often did cars pass by? About once a week!

We sat together to dinner, "Don't chew so noisily," Mr.Dharmasingha kept saying, staring at me. "Don't talk so loudly at table," he warned Gunadasa. "And don't make such a mess of your fingers. You should only use the tips of your fingers to mix your rice and curry, there shouldn't be anything on your fingers above the second digit. The moment Somalatha heard him say this she began to knead her food with her whole hand. When her parents forbade something she did it even more energetically.

Mr.Dharmasingha's preaching annoyed me no end. I felt very guilty about it until I was relieved to find that Somalatha and Gunadasa thought exactly as I did.

"I feel like mashing all the rice up when he goes on like that about it," said Gunadasa.

"Is it so bad to laugh at the table? Asked Somalatha.

"I don't know really….. I suppose it is."

Every full moon day we were made to recite from the Pali Scriptures and learn some stanzas by heart. Sometimes Mr. Dharmasingha translated them into Sinhala and explained them to us. I understood the stanzas about killing, lying and stealing perfectly, but there were one or two that defeated me completely. Mr.Dharmasingha lost his temper when he couldn't make us understand the Third Precept even though he went back to it month after month. I was able to learn the verses off by heart quite easily, but Gunadasa and Somalatha were hopeless.

"I will endeavour to refrain from unlawful sexual relationships......Mr.Dharmasingha repeated.

We said the words after him, in chorus.

"You know the meaning of 'I will refrain from unlawful sexual relationships', don't you? Mr. Dharmasingha asked looking at me.

It was Greek to me. The headmaster always translated this precept with downcast eyes. Sometimes he looked at me, but never at his own children. If his wife was there she always left us hurriedly at this point. I began to feel that this was some foul obscenity put into words that we could never understand.

"It is a deadly sin. Young as you are you must make up your minds never to fall into it." Said Mr.Dharmasingha.

"What is a deadly sin?" I asked.

"I'll explain some other time," said Mr. Dharmasingha getting up from the chair and becoming very busy about something.

"What does, refraining from unlawful sexual relationships, mean? How should we avoid it?" Gunadasa asked me.

"I don't know. It must be something really filthy," I said.

There were lots of toads and frogs in the ditches on either side of the house. Nine times out of ten if you turned over a stone you would find a toad under it. Sometimes after a sudden shower swarms of *meru* fluttered about the garden and the frogs would come out to jump at the *meru* and swallow them whole.

One Sunday evening we were catching small frogs by turning over stones in the garden. We got four little frogs into a coconut shell and put another shell over it as a lid. We took them to my room and let them go. "Ee!" said Somalatha running out of the door.

Let's have some fun," I suggested. We took the frogs into the dining room, put them on the table, and covered them with a flat clay *hatty*.

"Mother will thrash us," said Gunadasa.

It was soon time for tea. There was a plate of *helapa* and a bunch of ripe plantains on a white plate and of course, our *hatty*. Gunadasa looked at me furtively. I could see he was scared. Somalatha was trying to hide an impish smile.

"What's under this?:" said Mr.Dharmasingha lifting the *hatty*.

"What....!" He jumped away from the table dropping the *hatt*y. It smashed to the floor breaking into a thousand pieces. There were frogs all over the table.

Somalatha burst over laughing. Gunadasa was too frightened to laugh. Mr.Dharmasingha slapped Somalatha and she ran to her room crying, he dragged Gunadasa to the children's room, flung him in and locked the door. He caught me by the ear and pushed me into the other room. I heard him lock the door and take away the key.

There was a small connecting door between the rooms. I called Somalatha through the keyhole and they both came running to the door.

"Can't you get in here?" They begged.

"How can I? The door is locked and there's no key.

"The key was lost long ago. Try to break the lock," said Gunadasa.

"Too difficult. Wait. I'll try something else."

I searched the room carefully. I found a screwdriver in the drawer of a rickety old table and I tried it on the screws holding the hinges. They wouldn't budge. I tried tapping on the hinges.

"What are you doing?" They asked.

"Quiet"

Luckily there was a little coconut oil in a bottle in a corner. I put some oil around the screws of the top hinges and tried again. I had to try five times before I managed to get the screws off. I put the table against the door to hold it up and then pulled it back slowly. The other hinges began to give way. I got a pillow from the bed and laid it on the floor by the door and then pulled the door away. The hinge gave way and the door came down without a sound on the pillow. Somalatha ran across the door as if it were a bridge and then ran back again enjoying this new game.

I went into the other room. Somalatha hugged me in her excitement.

I tried Mr.Dharmasingha's *almariya*. It was locked.

"The key is in the drawer," said Somalatha, pulling out the long drawer below the doors.

"Let's have some fun, " I said.

"What?"

"We'll make a swing."

"Where's the rope?"

"We'll tie some of these together," I said pulling out a couple of tablecloths.

"Mother is sure to beat us," said Somalatha.

"We'll put them back before she come in."

I pulled out two tablecloths and two of Mrs.Dharmasingha's sarees and tied them end to end. I got Gunadasa to hold one end while I twisted them into a rope. Then we brought out Gunadasa's desk and put a chair on it. Gunadasa held the chair by the legs while I climbed on to it and tied the ends of the rope we had made to a rafter.

We had put Somalatha on the swing, and were pushing her when Mrs.Dharmasingha came in.

"*Apoi!*" she shouted, running to the door lying on the floor. "Who did this? Even the hinges….. Which of you did this?"

Then she saw the swing. "Apoi! Two of my sarees ruined! And two tablecloths! What have you done!"

She grabbed Somalatha and Gunadasa and dragged them away glowing at me.

"The boy is a real *Porisadaya*! If he stays here much longer there'll be nothing left of the house!"

She made so much noise that Mr.Dharmasingha came running in. He stopped aghast, staring, holding his head with his hands. He pulled my ears and shook me violently and slapped me left and right. He let me go only to run for the cane. I ran out of the room through the kitchen and out through the back door. There wasn't time to make for the gate. I ran to the back fence and jumped over it to escape the headmaster.

When I didn't return home that night Mr. Dharmasingha began to search for me with some men. I watched them looking into thickets, nooks and corners. Before they reached one hiding place I crept away to another. I heard later that they had scouted every lane, backyard and thicket. Mr.Dharmasingha had been heard telling his wife over and over again "If that scamp has an accident I will have to answer for it."

I watched the search party returning home after their unsuccessful expedition. They went out again after dinner. I heard them talking about looking for me along the seashore and in the bazaar next, and so I stayed hidden in the woods until they had gone to the seashore. When they went off towards the bazaar I went down to the beach. The moonlit beach and sky were beautiful. Some fishermen came down to the beach with their oars, torches and sacks and set off to sea in two of the canoes. They were going to the reef where they would light their torches and fish all night.

I climbed into one of the big seagoing boats drawn up on the beach and lay in the stern. I could hear the murmuring of the sea and the talk of two more fishermen who had come down to their boat. Lulled by the sea breeze I soon went to sleep.

I was awakened by the rocking of the boat. The sun had risen. I heard a creaking and the sound of voices.

"*Menna bung*! There's someone here. I felt something move under my feet!"

I found two eyes staring down at me out of a bearded face. I couldn't think where I was, and I jumped to my feet.

"*Menna!* There's a boy in the boat!"

"A boy! *Deiyyo sakki*" cried the helmsman opening his eyes wide in amazement. The fishermen hadn't seen me till then because they had set off before dawn.

"What mischief could he have been up to? We're too far out now. We can't go back now to put him ashore, we'd lose our fishing today."

"Throw the rascal into the sea and let's keep going," said one of the oarsmen angrily.

"Why that's the boarder at the headmaster's." said another man.

I was relieved that someone had recognized me.

"That schoolmaster is a miserly old *kuna*," said another.

"You don't have to take me back," I said. "Let me come with you. I'll do whatever you say. I'll do any work you want. I'm not scared."

"He's a tough nut all right," said the man who had wanted to throw me into the sea.

The helmsman had to decide. It was obvious that there wasn't enough time to take me back and get back to their fishing.

"The boy isn't scared. Let him come with us to the *hantena*," said the man who had recognized me.

I was thrilled when the helmsman agreed. We were out of sight of land and I thought we must be in the middle of the ocean. I could see nothing but the sea on all sides; the sky above was like a huge sapphire bowl. The fishermen were still steering by a landmark, a hill that looked like a tiny cloud on the horizon. When that, too, disappeared they went by the light of the Devundara lighthouse.

A steady breeze sprang up and the men shipped their oars, while one of them shook out the sail. He tied one end to the crossbeam and then the helmsman took charge. The boat really began to move now. The fishermen were amazed to see me standing firm in the middle of the boat, holding on to the end of a pole. The helmsman said that even a fisherman wouldn't have been so fearless on his first trip to the *bala* grounds. The boat went hissing through the water and we were soon at the *hantena*.

The men let down their stone anchor slowly. They called it the *pânagala* and the sea around the *hentena* the *pitigala*.

When they cast anchor I was able to stop holding on and to clamber about the boat, helping the men. They tied their sacks at their waists and took up their huge bamboo fishing rods. I handed a sack to one and a water "bottle" to another. Two of them got out the bait of red *ingura* and began to throw it into the sea like farmers sowing grain. The sea around the boats began to look like a red cloth and the *balaya* came jumping and fighting for the bait, churning the water. The fishermen held their rods against their hips with one hand and threw their lines into the water with the other. Their sacks were ready, tied to their waists. They had hardly thrown in their lines when they were pulling away the rods, for the *balaya* were leaping for the bait. And so they went on throwing and jerking back their lines, a *balaya* falling into the boat with each pull. I could hear the thudding all round me as the fish were dropped into the boat.

The sea was a battle field. *Balaya* were even banging against the sides of the boat. They fought for the bait like a pack of dogs for bones or like bats around a fruit tree…. The noise was that of huge bellows at work together with a violent slapping sound as if people were thrashing about wildly in the water.

I've never been in anything so fascinating, so exciting, since I think the fishermen too, loved the thrill of it more than a gambler loves his game. Compared even with the smallest of ships a sea going canoe is no better than a bit of bark. These men go far out to sea in them facing unimaginable dangers. A sudden gale could send them no one knows where; a big wave could destroy both men and boat, they could be dashed to pieces on the rocks. Clinging to the wreckage rarely saves them, it is all too likely that they would starve to death if cast adrift on the vast watery deserts of the ocean.

Do they venture out beyond the horizon merely because this is their livelihood? I think they love the life itself. I can say this because I had that chance to see them pulling in the *balaya* and *kelawalla*. I remember the looks on their faces and the things they talked about.

The boat was full of fish in half an hour. Perhaps the men thought the boat would be swamped if they took any more fish for they stopped work and sat down to eat their rice. They were in fine spirits. One of the men said he wouldn't mind sharing with me and many of the others echoed him.

"But he won't be able to eat such hot stuff," said one.

"Oh, no, I'm quite used to it," I said. "Sometimes when we were out playing in our village I've eaten *maniocca* with *pol sambala*."

They washed their hands in the sea and untied their bundles. The helmsman who had the best and biggest meal, shared it with me. I've never had a meal I enjoyed more. The sea air had made me hungry and I was still full of the excitement of watching the fishing. *Samba* rice, *balaya* cooked dry in the *ambul thial* style and pol *sambola* made a better meal than the most expensive food I've eaten with a dozen dishes of fish, meat and vegetable. I hadn't had anything to eat all night and even in the morning, and I quickly finished everything I'd been given. Another man gave me a bit more rice and the helmsman gave me some *sambola*, smiling to see how hungry I was. I washed my hands in the sea when I finished, and drank some water out of a coconut shell.

The helmsman took a straw pouch from his waist and began to chew a quid of betel. The others followed suit. "Do you chew betel? Asked one, offering me some.

"Did you like the fishing?" Asked the helmsman.

"Yes, very much, I wish I could come again."

"Aha!" said the fisherman, laughing.

"You're not to come near the boat again. Do you hear?"

"You didn't know, boy – there are times we have been sorry we didn't bring fewer men. Two or three less and we could take in more fish! Did you see how the fish were tumbling in?"

He related a story about a *Kachcheri Mudaliyar* who wanted to see the *bala* fishing. He was so determined that the fishermen had to take him, for such officials could be very useful to them. They had come upon a huge shoal of *balaya* and the boat was soon full of fish. The fishermen could have taken sixty or seventy more *balaya* but for the *Kachcheri Mudaliyar*.

"Throw the fellow into the sea and let's take another hundred *balaya*," one of the men had said murderously.

I'm sure the story was invented to poke fun at the greed of fishermen, but the man enjoyed telling it!

"Time to go back," said the helmsman.

They hauled in the anchor and the boat began to move quickly landwards.

For a long time I could see nothing but a vast stretch of water wherever I looked. The boat was like an ant crawling painfully across a blue cloth. After a while a little smudge like a cloud came into sight over the horizon.

"There's our landmark," said the helmsman.

The cloud rose and expanded and I saw that it was a hill covered with trees. The dark smudges gradually took shape as trees. After a while we could make out the coconut palms and the huts along the beach. There were canoes drawn up in a row on the beach. Soon I saw crows fighting over bait thrown away by the fishermen. My pleasure began to ebb, for I remembered Mr. Dharmasingha, I knew that the headmaster's house wasn't far from the beach.

We went ashore at about three o'clock in the afternoon. Men and boys came running to peep into the boat. One of the men recognized me as I jumped out.

"*Deiyo sakki*! Mr. Dharmasingha has been looking for you everywhere!"

"That's a very clever boy," said the helmsman. I realized that the fishermen were superstitious about the good luck they had and liked me better for it. They ought to take me with them every time they went after balaya!

The helmsman called one of the fisherman to him.

"Take this boy to headmaster Dharmasingha's and give them two of the *balaya*."

The headmaster and his wife gave sighs of relief when they saw me. Somalatha looked at me with tear-dimmed eyes. Gunadasa was full of admiration for my exploit as he asked me, "Did you go far out to sea?"

"So you have been to sea, have you? To bring us these fish, no doubt!" said Mrs.Dharmasingha. A fine thing you've done! Our minds were on fire all the time. You turned our blood to water, It's we who have to answer to your father!"

Mr.Dharmasingha didn't say a word. Somalatha and Gunadasa came to ask me all about my adventures, but I was so tired that I just dropped into bed and fell asleep.

The next day Mr.Dharmasingha and his wife told father the whole story. It was only then that I discovered that the headmaster had sent father a telegram as soon as I'd come ashore.

"In spite of all the mischief he's been up to we've never even touched him, I heard Mrs.Dharmasingha say.

"You should thrash him – yes thrash him well and truly! Didn't I tell the headmaster right at the start to thrash him if he didn't behave? There's no changing him if you don't thrash him soundly!"

"How could we do that? He's your son, after all. I just couldn't do it."

"Thrash him, headmaster, thrash him, I won't take it amiss, whatever you do."

"Please take him home with you, *Mudalali Mahattaya*. We would like you to take him away."

"How can I do that now – didn't you say that the exam is quite near? Please forgive him this time and let him stay on."

"The boy has been here for a year hasn't he? He's only become more unruly than ever. Well – I suppose I can't refuse you. I'll keep him until the exams are over."

"I'll never forget your kindness."

Mrs.Dharmasingha began to sing father's praises.

"We know, *Mudalali Mahattaya*…. We understand that you're no miser when it comes to educating this boy. There's no reason why he shouldn't do well. He has brains all right. His only defect is his unruliness."

"You can only set that right by thrashing him. Beat him well, Mrs.Dharmasingha. I won't complain even if you draw blood."

"*Aney*, how could we possibly beat him? But I nearly lost my temper when I found he had torn up two of my best sarees. Yet! I didn't scold him even then. You can ask the child whether I'm telling the truth."

"Would I ever do that? I wish you had beaten him soundly. You won't bring him round if you don't."

"No….. we never beat even our own children. I couldn't bring myself to do it. But I am rather hurt that he ruined my best sarees."

"I'm sorry, I forgot to pay for the sarees," said father, pulling out his purse and giving her thirty rupees. "Please buy two new sarees. And don't hesitate to thrash him next time."

"How can we beat a son of yours?" She repeated taking the thirty rupees with a show of reluctance.

"There's no need to pay for them," she said. But she didn't hand the money back.

"No you must take the money."

"Only because you insist…." Mrs.Dharmasingha tucked the money into her waist carefully.

# CHAPTER IV

# THE FIGHT

Father refused to take me home that Sinhala New Year. He wanted me to stay on at the headmaster's to study for the examination.

If it wasn't for the two children it would have been as bad as living in a deserted house. The headmaster and his wife spent their time joylessly doing the same old things – going to school and back daily, spending the rest of their time until they went to bed, shouting at us "Don't do that, don't laugh so noisily, don't hurt that animal," hoarding money like termites building an ant-hill, counting five rupees over and over before they parted with the money. Such life as there was in the headmaster must have been shriveling up steadily, like the kernel's of those coconuts that villagers keep in their kitchen lofts for years and years.

I spent most of the time playing outside with my school friends until I was ready to drop. Somalatha and Gunadasa were not allowed to go far from home. Perhaps the headmaster let me go where I wanted only because he was afraid of the damage we might do to the furniture and the crockery if I too was forced to spend all that time about the house.

On the first day of the Sinhala New Year festival the auspicious guest was one of the shop-keepers. Mr.Dharmasingha had chosen him because he thought it would be especially lucky to receive the auspicious coins from the hands of a money-maker. We all sat on mats spread on the floor, as everyone was supposed to do, and ate the first meal off plantain leaves at the auspicious time. A little later, the shop-keeper arrived. He sat at the table, on which had been placed a dish of milk-rice, plateful of various New Year foods, and a brass oil-lamp. He rolled a little of the milk-rice into a ball and put it into the oil-lamp, which had already been lit. He put a one cent coin beside it. He then gave each of us a silver coin and a copper wrapped up in a betel leaf. The headmaster and his wife took the whole thing very seriously. Mr.Dharmasingha locked his gift away, the old lady treated hers with the reverence we give a sacred relic. I wonder if she burned incense before it? I heard that they didn't touch these gifts until the next Sinhala New Year.

Gunadasa and I were each given a ten cent coin and a one cent coin. Somalatha was given a five cent coin and a cent. After the shopkeeper had left Mr.Dharmasingha, too, gave each of us a coin wrapped in a betel leaf. We got together to examine our presents.

"Mine's a cent, "said Gunadasa

I showed them what I had.

"That's a cent too!" exclaimed Somalatha. "Don't you spend that money now," said Mrs. Dharmasingha."You must keep it wrapped in the betel leaf until the New Year comes round again."

# THE FIGHT

Somalatha immediately began to chew her betel leaf. I loved to see her doing exactly the opposite of everything she was told to do by the Dharmasinghas.

We were allowed to play for money only on New year's day. On any other day we would be punished for it by Mrs.Dharmasingha. Many of our friends came to play with us. Among them was Piyadasa, the boy who nicknamed me *Galibba*.

We played *Gadol Manima* with our coins. I kept winning, while Somalatha was losing steadily. I watched to see why. The next time she threw her coin it fell almost in the centre of one of the squares. It would be hard to make a better throw. I kept watch. I saw Piyadasa edging the coin away from the centre of the square with his foot. Perhaps he didn't want Somalatha to win because he's seen her borrowing money from me. I went up to him and kicked him in the shin. He hit me, and I hit back. But then the other children rushed between and pulled us apart.

We dropped *Gadol Manima* after that and started "*Catch the Fly*". We each put a coin on the floor and then we stood quietly, watching. The owner of the coin on which the fly settled first was the winner, and he got all the coins. Piyasena won five times in a row. Then two others won. I noticed that Piyasena was careful to keep back the coin he put down and hand over another coin to the winner.

Why did he do that? How had he won five times in a row?

A fly settled on Piyasena's coin for the sixth time. I grabbed it, looked at both sides carefully and then I got it! It was stinking of rotten dried fish! I asked another boy to smell it.

"It smells of *Karawala*," he said and threw it down. Piyasena saw the others, too, stooping for the coin and he jumped on it and began rubbing it hard on the floor with his foot. I pushed him away roughly and picked up the coin again. The smell was much less now.

Piyasena was furious. He hit me with his clenched fist so violently that I could barely keep my feet. But I soon got over the pain and shock and went for him. He hit me again, and then the others pushed him away and saved me. He struggled to get at me and this annoyed the other boys. They set on him, so vigorous that he was forced to break free and run away.

He must have kept his coin in a bag of *Karawala* for at least a day! The, boys nicknamed him "*Karawalaya*".

After the New year, Mr. Dharmasingha made his class work harder than ever. The exams were quite close now. I wondered why he took so much trouble, for we thought him a nuisance and even made fun of him. He wasn't content just to earn his salary he really loved teaching, and it kept him going despite all his old-fashioned ways.

Most of us did learn quite a lot of Arithmetic, Grammar, Composition and History. I hate studying, so if I know anything at all, it's because Mr.Dharmasingha was such a good teacher. Even though he was taking such pains he became very nervous and excited as the day came nearer. He was particularly worried about our dictation, he was sure we would not remember when to write the "dental" and "cerebral" versions of *na* and *la*. Examiners always pay special attention to these letters. The headmaster knew that even scholars who knew Pali and Sanskrit could not always be sure which letters to use. Only masters of etymology and classical prose could be expected to get them right every time.

The headmaster decided to use a trick. He told us "when the dictation is given I will scratch my head whenever you ought to write a cerebral letter".

When the day came the dictation was given by the headmaster himself. We looked at him slyly whenever we came to a *na* or *la* and everything went perfectly!

## CHAPTER V

# THE CONFIDENCE TRICK

Eight months after the exams, Mr.Dharmasingha was transferred to the school at Dickwella and I had to go back to our village. At first I thought he had been transferred because the trick he taught us for dictation had been found out. But I heard later that he had asked for the transfer himself.

In fact, I think he wanted to leave Welikanda simply to get rid of me without offending father. After my adventure at sea he left me alone and didn't scold me any more. Indeed, he rarely even spoke to me. He obviously didn't want to have anything to do with me.

Father took me back to the school in our village. He was afraid if I wasn't sent to school I would get worse and worse.. That was why he didn't take me in to his shop straight away. I found out later that he wanted to apprentice me to a trader in the hills after I passed the Grade Eight examination.

Jinna, Ranadeva, Dangadasa and Siripala welcomed me back enthusiastically. But my stepmother wasn't at all pleased to see me. I don't think she was jealous of me. But I have to admit that I'd become a nuisance to her and my father.

I had often heard tales of the exploits of a villager called Suranchiya…. He was also called *Colomba-rala.* I imagined him to be a sort of super bandit. Born in our village, he had left for Colombo when he was still a boy of ten, the villagers said. He had become a famous thief. They said that he used to break into the houses of white men, wearing a mask, and carry away spoons, forks, table knives, clocks, silver picture frames and so on,. They believed that he knew a spell which he muttered thrice over and then all he had to do was to breathe on his palm and press it against a door for it to swing open. He would come to the village sometimes with a load of stolen goods. He stayed at his aunt's house for a few days and then went back to Colombo. The last time had been about ten years ago. He had given the villagers presents of silver spoons and ivory handled knives and had given the headman's son a watch. He had given the headman himself a dozen silver spoons and table knives. He sold the other things he had to the richer villagers and then went off to Colombo again.But he had managed by then to get back the watch and take twenty five rupees off the headman as well. He had first got the headman to lend him twenty five rupees and then told the sone secretly, "one of my friends has tipped me off that the police are going to search the village. Some enemy of your father has told the police that you and your father are selling stolen goods here. Don't keep that watch on you, the name of the European to whom it belongs is engraved on it. Give it to me, I'll hide it until the police give up searching for it."

Two days later Suranchiya disappeared. That same day a policeman came to the headman's house and questioned him about Suranchiya. Some villagers are sure that this wasn't a policeman at all but one of Suranchiya's accomplices in disguise. Others say that the story was invented by those who didn't get any presents from Suranchiya and that he was really a friend of the poor. I believed the villagers who made him out to be a bandit hero.

To our surprise and delight Suranchiya suddenly appeared in the village. He was almost a six-footer dark as a black bear and with a crow's nest of jet black hair. I don't know why his face with its sharp eyes reminded me of a jackal or of the eyes and beak of a hawk. I'd expected to see a giant with upturned moustache but our admiration remained as great as ever. He wore a black shirt, a black scarf tied round his waist and a silk sarong which swished against his ankles as he walked.

He made friends with the children at once. He gave me a new tennis ball, something we rarely even saw and a knife with four blades, a corkscrew and a sharp little spike. I wrapped the knife in a piece of cloth and put it away in an *almariya* under one of my stepmother's silk clothes.

Suranchiya often came to the woods to watch us playing or to tell us amazing stories about his life in Colombo.

When he broke into a house he repeated a sleeping spell three times and blew thrice into the air. Everybody in the house immediately went into a deep sleep and Suranchiya was able to put all their knives, forks, clocks, silver vases and trays into his big bag and just walk away! As soon as he got out of the house he changed his disguise once again.....

"Do you get into houses by repeating a spell three times and putting your palm against the door? I asked.

He promptly told us more about his adventures. He had once got into an estate bungalow in the hills and had collected all the silver in the cupboards into his bag. He was just making his escape through the hall when a large dog sprang at him, barking furiously. Suranchiya threw a piece of meat to the dog and the dog began to eat the meat, but the Tamil servant had been roused by the barking. They were running here and there shouting *"kallen! kallen!"* Immediately Suranchiya who was in disguise had joined them shouting *"kallen! kallen!* with the rest.

"What is the meaning of *"kallen, kallen*?" I asked him. "It means"thief,thief!"

After about a week Suranchiya went to Colombo and came back with a pretty woman. He introduced her everywhere as "the actress, Annie Perera." He said that she was a great actress whose tragic songs always made women and children weep while the men stared at her in admiration and slyly sent her presents the next day.

Suranchiya's stories about the actress made us look at her as if she was a heroine. Even the villagers were thrilled by these stories and they soon began to repeat them as if they had seen her performances themselves. When she stepped out of doors she was always heavily powdered, and her lips were reddened, she wore silk jackets and clothes and high heeled shoes.

Suranchiya and the actress went to see the Manager of the school to engage the school hall for a performance. Suranchiya said he had written the play himself. The Manager was so impressed by Suranchiya and his companion that he let them have the hall the next Saturday free of charge.

Suranchiya and the actress went back to Colombo the next day. Within two days he was back with a sheaf of handbills. He got us to distribute the handbills everywhere in the village and in the neighbouring villages too. He gave the five of us free seats and promised us presents after the show. The handbills read;

THE CONFIDENCE TRICK

## MAGADI NATAKAYA

The world –famous ANNIE PERERA will
Appear as

**Princess Suvinitha**
Songs sweeter than the singing of Kokilayas!

**Prince    Valentine**

Steals the key from the mouth of the demon
Who guards the cave, rescues the
Princess and

## FLIES THROUGH THE AIR

Magical! Unbelievable! Wonderful!

## AMAZING!

See the sorcerer staked alive!
Commit pieces by the
famous comedian

## BAMANADASA!

Rates: Armchairs Rs.1/50, Chairs -/75 cts.
Benches -/25 cts.
**Stage Manager: Manimel Perera**

This handbill excited us so much that we could scarcely
wait for the day. We each had a handbill hidden among our
school books.

"We couldn't understand "Commit pieces by
Bamandasa." No one in the village could explain this line. In
the end we went to Suranchiya himself.

"Commit means 'funny'; 'commit pieces' are funny
scenes," he said.

The headman's son knew English. He didn't like Suranchiya and he scoffed at the phrase. :Commit pieces! The buffaloes! Who doesn't know the word 'comic'?" he said with an air of learning.

On Sunday evening Suranchiya came looking for me. He took the knife back.

"There are two letters engraved on it," he said." It won't be safe for you to keep it. The C.I.D. has got news of the play. They are looking for me, and they might search the village for stolen goods. I'll keep the knife with me for a bit. I'll give it back when it's safe."

The school hall was packed that Saturday night. There were even ten or twelve women. The benches were crowded with young men and boys. Two big kerosene lamps lighted the stage.

But there was no sign of the play starting. The crowd was getting very restless. "What's the delay! People began to ask. Some of the young men began whistling with their fingers in their mouth.

"What's happening? Is the *Magadi Natakaya* a real *magadiya*? Someone shouted.

"Ey! If you can't get started give our money back!" shouted another.

The children began to thump on the benches and even the people in the armchairs were getting annoyed.

There was a sudden noise in the dressing room. We could hear people hitting each other. The commotion increased, as if a pack of bulls were battling backstage. We heard shouting. The women sprang up in alarm and some of the men surrounded them as if to protect them. There was a crash of furniture and a man with an open wound came rushing out.

"The actors are fighting each other! They are real desperadoes…they won't stop till someone gets killed. Run! Run!, for your lives…." He disappeared into the darkness.

Everybody followed him. Some of the women, were screaming. We too ran with the others. We stopped only half a mile away.

The man with the wound wasn't one of the villagers. We saw some of the young men going back to the school and we followed them. Two policemen were pushing Suranchiya into a buggy.

"Ey! Give back the money!" shouted one of the young men.

"Money" laughed one of the policemen. "This fellow broke into the house of an Englishman. He has stolen silver spoons and forks and knives, gold watches and diamond rings! We found a watch and a clasp knife in the dressing room. We have arrested him. If you want to make a complaint against him you can come to the Police Station."

It was only the next day, that we discovered how we had been tricked. No actors from Colombo had come to our village, least of all the "World Famous" Annie Perera. Suranchiya and some of his gang had staged the whole thing and started the "fight" backstage. The man with the wound was one of these men. They had put some red dye on him. The policemen, too, were part of the gang. The real police had sent word to our headman, too late, that Suranchiya had worked the same trick on two other distant villages and collected a lot of money. The Inspector told the headman to inform him if Suranchiya showed up again.

"He took back the watch he gave me only that morning," said Dangadasa.

"Why did you let him?"

"He scared me into it. He said that a white man's initials were carved on it."

"The rogue took back my knife too! I said."

"What a trickster"

"He cheated us all!"

"But I still have the rubber ball!" I said.

# CHAPTER VI

# THE RAID

Though I still hated having to study I went to school regularly now. Father no longer punished me. But somehow I didn't like being back at home. When Suranchiya came to the village we had been completely won over by him, but our admiration disappeared when he tricked us. The villagers made fun of the people who had gone to the *Magadi Natakaya* but they left us alone.

School closed for the New Year holiday. Jinna and I played with the other boys all day. The grownups gave the children more freedom during the New Year season. This was the cadju season and the boys spent most of their time on the cadju trees. You could hardly find a cadju tree that had not been stripped bare. But there was one cadju orchard that we could never get into. It belonged to a former monk who wouldn't allow the children anywhere near his cadju trees. The branches were weighed down with bright red fruit and we kept watch hopelessly.

Early one morning Jinna came running with the news that he had seen Upasakappu going out somewhere dressed in white cloth and coat and carrying an umbrella.

"That means he'll be gone for some time – he usually wears only a cloth and *baniama.*"

"He won't be back before nightfall! Let's start on his cadju."

We went at once. It took us nearly a quarter of an hour to clear away the thorn bushes with which he had blocked up the gate. We were all very angry.

"We mustn't leave a single fruit on the trees," said Jinna.

I kept guard at the gate with Siripala. Jinna and Dangadasa climbed two of the trees and began to throw down the cadju. Ranadeva went round the trees with a basket, collecting the fruit they dropped. Jinna was on his third tree when I saw Upasakppu coming back. I shouted to Siripala to get out over the back fence. I picked up the basket and ran for the woods. Then I remembered that Jinna wouldn't have enough time to get down the tree and escape. The four of us went back to the fence and peeped in.

Upasakappu had collared Jinna. He was shaking in fury, and he shouted "Come to the police you... I saw him strike Jinna. "Come on," I shouted and we went over the fence and ran at him. I dived for his knees and the others pulled him this way and that. Jinna broke free and began to push Upasakappu. He went over backwards and we fell in a heap with him. The four others struggled to hold him down while I ran for a rope. We tied his hands together.

We got over the fence and made off into the woods though not before we'd picked up our basket and even the cadju that had fallen out on the grass.

Soon a story was sweeping through the village that we'd broken into Uapasakappu's house. "They had collected together

51

some money and valuables, but Upasakappu returned before they got away. Jinna hit him on the head with a *Kitul* club and then ran away with Upali," Upasakappu had not been able to recognize the other three boys.

This wasn't all. Upasakappu had gone to the police with his story. The police would be in the village any moment now. We were sure to be arrested.

Father thrashed Jinna and me that night. I overheard him telling my stepmother that Upasakappu must have pretended not to know who the other boys were because they were all close relatives of the headman.

"The boy's nearly fifteen* now. You can't reform him by thrashing him," said my stepmother.

"I'll send the fellow to Simon *Mudalai*; immediately," said father. "Simon told me to send the boy to him last month. He said he could teach him to work in a shop in a very short time. He won't be allowed out very often when he's working in a shop in the hills.....besides they'll make him do all the heavy work for a start."

"Yes, we've done our best to give him an education. If he doesn't care for that there's nothing more we can do. We have to hand him over to someone else, even if it means that he'll have to work as a labourer. He'll only get worse and worse if he stays here."

Though father didn't say anything about policemen coming to arrest us I was still as frightened as before. I was scared of being sent to Maskeliya. We thought of being sent to work in a shop in the hill country as a kind of imprisonment. We knew that boys in such shops had to work from seven in the morning to eight at night, that they had to carry heavy loads of salt, chillies and dried fish.

I decided to run away from home with Jinna. He agreed at once, for he was still afraid that the police might come for us.

After father and my stepmother had gone to sleep, I made a bundle of clothes to take with me. I took two sarongs, two shirts and a pair of short trousers. Jinna too, had rolled up a couple of sarongs and vests in an old newspaper. We stayed awake and left home soon   after midnight.

We had no plan and we decided to go where our feet led us. When we came to the road we saw two double- bullock carts heading for Galle and we decided to follow them.

The next morning we found ourselves twenty miles from the village. We sat in a dilapidated *ambalama* trying to think what to do next.

"Let's ask the owner of that copra shed for work" said Jinna.

"What kind of work?"

"Any kind…. Whatever we can. We can move on after a few days."

"Move on where?"

"Anywhere! We don't have to think so far ahead!"

The *Mudalali* took us on after questioning us a bit. He was full of sympathy, when we told him that we were two fatherless boys from Welimada. I had to keep watch over the copra spread out daily in the yard for sun drying and Jinna had to look after his cart bulls. We were sometimes asked to work in the house too.

"These two boys can't be from Welimada," I heard the *Mudalali's* wife tell her husband one day. "I'm sure they are Southerners, too."

We realized that we might fall into father's hands if we stayed on so near a main road. Two months had passed already. We decided to go deeper into the country. The *Mudalali* gave each of us three rupees a month, and we tucked the money away at our waists, We went on beyond Ataanikitta to Batavatukissa and found work with a *hena* farmer.

We felt that no one would ever find us here. We soon grew to like the valley which was teeming with porcupine, hare and wild boar. The farmer had two guns, a muzzle-loader and a breach-loader, and he taught me how to shoot at a mark. He found me an eager pupil; within six months I was a better shot than he. The first time I shot a wild boar Podi Gamarala laughed and said "Sinner!"

"Sinner? Am I the only one?" I asked.

"I rarely hit the animals I shoot at," he said." I learnt to handle a gun only because I wanted to scare animals away from the *hena*. I'm no good at shooting them. Only a sinner can become a good marksman."

Jinna and I helped him grow *batala* and *maniocca*. We like this kind of work, and although Podi Gamarala didn't encourage the killing of animals he was pleased that I was protecting his crops. When we returned tired and hungry from the *hena* at midday, the meals of rice, *maniocca* and curried dry fish were the best I've ever had, except once. That was when I went to sea the day I ran away from Mr.Dharmasingha.

Podi Gamarala's *hena* lay on the far side of the Koggala river. Not far away was the Pambanam-Ela, a small watercourse which was full of crocodiles. The villagers told such terrible stories about these crocodiles that I thought I would take a canoe down the Pambanam Ela one day to see them for myself. They were supposed to pull even full grown bulls into the water if they wandered to the river side to drink. Only recently a crocodile had torn the arm off a villager who had gone into the water.

Not far from our *hena* there was an island in the middle of the river. The people called it *Madol Doova*. Of all the innumerable islands, of this reach of the Koggala river *Madol Doova* had a particularly evil reputation for being densely forested and infested with snakes. People from villages on either side of the river had used it for a long time as a dumping ground for cobras, vipers, *mapillas* and every other kind of poisonous snake. They didn't want to kill the snakes, so when one was found near a house they caught it in a mat bag, rowed out to *Madol Doova* and threw the bag ashore.

People also believed that the island was haunted by various devils and this was another reason why nobody ever went there; even the fishermen who went out at night made a point of avoiding it. *Madol Doova* was supposed to have been the home of gangs of bandits in the times of the ancient kings and there were tales of fabulous robbers dens made by the bandits among the rocks and of a strange pool in the middle of the island.

Everybody said that quite recently a ghostly figure carrying fire on its head had been seen walking on the island. But I couldn't find a single man in any of the villages by the river who had been on the island.

The stories I heard made me more and more curious and eager to go to the island. Jinna and I often rowed past it but we hadn't set foot on it. Jinna who usually followed me in everything, wouldn't hear of going ashore, probably because he believed all the stories he had heard.

"Don't ever set foot on that island," said Podi Gamarala when he heard of my curiosity. "It's a den of snakes and besides, its haunted.

One evening I took our boat out secretly without letting even Jinna know. I paddled across the river and moored it near the shore of *Madol Doova*. The moment I stepped out of the boat I sank to my knees in mud. I had a hard time pulling myself free.

The shallows were shaded over by dense growth of *Kadol* and *Kirala* trees and clumps of the huge *keran* fern. The tops of the ferns looked like giant centipedes, the huge prop roots of the *Kirala* trees were like iron spikes sunk in the water to keep off intruders. I hacked my way through the thick ferns to gain a high rock and looked around me. Although the skirts of the island were thickly forested there was one place in the centre where the trees were few. I saw two or three coconut trees in the open space and some wild mango trees heavy with fruit. Who could have planted coconut trees in the middle of the island? People must have lived here fifty or sixty years ago. I forced my way through the undergrowth to the coconut trees. Dry coconuts lay where they had fallen under the trees and there were overripe mangoes every where.

The shrieks of parrots and bats around the mango and cadju trees were ear-splitting. The sudden cry of a *Kerella* sounded like a mocking laugh intended for me.

Just when I turned to go back I heard a sound like a man clearing his throat some distance away. I stopped dead and listened but I didn't hear anything unusual. I hawked and spat and called out "Who's there!" but there was no response. I wondered if the island really was haunted. I was determined to go back to the island soon. I put two coconuts I had picked up into the boat and paddled back home.

Jinna was impatient to go to the island, too, when I told him what I had done. We went together a week later and explored one side of the island. We couldn't get to the other side because there was thick jungle right across the island and no tracks anywhere. But on one side we found a cave and a pond. There were many signs that the cave had been fixed up for living in by a stonemason. There was room inside for three people to sleep comfortably. The floor had been made as smooth as a slate. We couldn't see how the cave came to be so bright, there was as much light there as outside.

"Let's live on the island and start a *hena*, " I said.

"How can we get food?"

"We must have pots and pans, we must bring everything we might need. When we finish what we have brought we can take the boat across for more."

56

"We won't be able to clear this jungle without axes and knives and *udellas.*"

We'll buy some. We don't need a house, we can live in the cave. If we clean up the pond we won't need a well."

We went back and told Podi Gamarala about *Madol Doova.*

"Are there any cobras and vipers?" he asked.

"We didn't see a single!"

"What?"

"Not even a harmless rat snake. There might be snakes in the jungle, of course."

" I always thought you couldn't even set foot on *Madol Doova* without treading on a snake!" he said wonderingly. "What happens to all the snakes put there by the people around here?"

"How are the snakes to get out of those bags?" Perhaps they die inside! And some might even have swum back to their homes. But there's plenty of food for snakes!"

"Can snakes swim that far?" asked Jinna.

"Yes" said Podi Gamarala.

He gave us an old canoe, some pots and a stone mortar. We used eight of our twelve rupees to buy rice, salt, chillies and other stocks, and also two large knives and two plates. Podi Gamarala also gave us two *udellas* and a pruning knife, and we borrowed one of his axes.

# CHAPTER VII

# MADOL DOOVA

We spent two days repairing the canoe, turning it over and stopping up the leaks with fibre, gum and melted resin. We replaced the poles joining the outrigger to the canoe and overhauled the outrigger. One Sunday morning we floated the canoe and loaded it with our things. Podi Gamarala presented us with a well-grown pup and his breach-loader.

"The load is a bit too much," he said. "Be careful how you row."

We set off, going very slowly, and headed for the southern tip of the island. This time we hit on a better place for going ashore. There were outcrops of rock and hardly any mud. The *Kadol* stilt roots were like a bridge girdling the island. We disembarked, carried our things ashore and beached the canoe. We rolled some logs and stones and built ourselves a small pier.

We cleaned up the cave and put our mats, pillows and other stuff inside. After a short rest we cut down the undergrowth to make a foot-path from the cave to our pier. We made a scrap meal of coconuts and later had some *kapu* fruits.

When night fell, Jinna cooked some rice. I scraped some coconut and made a coconut *sambala*. We had a big meal and then spread our mats on the floor of the cave. We fell asleep as soon as we lay down and awoke only when the birds began their songs the next morning Birds were singing everywhere. I heard notes I'd never heard before. It was like a whole orchestra of flutes, *udeki, veenas* and conches sounding off together.

We went down to the pier for a wash and after breakfast of boiled *batala* we went up to the clear space near the coconut trees. We pulled up the weeds and shrubs there and loosened up the soil. The next day we laid our beds and planted *maniocca* and *batala* cuttings. The day after we picked mangoes, split them in half, scored lines in the flesh, salted them and put them on a rock to dry.

Within two weeks we managed to make a cheerful home for ourselves. We cleaned out the pond and repaired its sides with stones we carried up.

One evening, that second week, Jinna and I were outside our cave. He was lying on a rock and I was sitting on another not far away when he called to me.

"Upali *Mahattaya*....look!"

Through the trees we could see a light dipping and rising on the other side of the island.

"There it is! The light's going down....there, it's rising now.....it's moving again!"

I, too could see the light moving up and down quite clearly.

"Remember that Podi Gamarala told us there was a ghost on that side of the island?" Jinna asked me.

I had never been very interested in ghost stories, not even when I was very young. I hadn't thought much about whether there were ghosts or not. Perhaps I have only thought about ghosts when I had to go at night through a thick jungle or past a cemetery. I wasn't scared by Jinna's discovery, only curious.

"We can't get through this jungle now. We can't do it even in daytime." I said. "Shall we get into the canoe and go round to the other side?"

"We'll only smash up the boat if we try that now in the dark," said Jinna. "There are rocks everywhere on that side. Don't you remember Podi Gamarala telling us that you can't take a boat round there?"

We climbed up to a high rock and looked across the island. Something was moving across the river on the other side. It was a canoe. If it was impossible to take a boat to the other side of the island why was someone doing it at this time in the dark? There was some mystery here. I told Jinna how I'd thought I heard a man clearing his throat the first day I had come to the island.

We were running out of food, so the next day we went across to Podi Gamaral's plot taking with us some of the dried mangoes and some cadjunuts. He would only take some of the mangoes. We took the rest to the village and sold enough to be able to buy rice, some salt and chillies and so on. I bought some fishing lines and hooks too, for I wanted to try the fishing off the island. After eating the mid-day meal with Podi Gamarala we went back to the island.

We began cutting a path through the jungle next morning. It was hard going, for the undergrowth was thick with thorn bushes and creepers. *Eraminiya* bushes, *Katukurundu* trees, *Pathok*, *Navahandi* and such plants were everywhere.

That evening Jinna began putting down some seeds we had been given by Podi Gamarala. He made beds of *bandakka, vatakolu, pathola* and a few other vegetables, while I cut down a *kitul* palm and made a fishing rod with the tackle we had bought. I fished from a rock by the riverside and after a while Jinna came over to watch. I caught three *Gombataya* and a large *Iribataya* and Jinna skinned and cooked them. We had fish curry for dinner that night.

We worked at the path through the jungle for two weeks without getting very far. Besides, our eagerness grew less when we didn't see the floating fire any more. We began to see that the jungle was only getting thicker and thicker and that we hadn't even got halfway. We began to spend more time on our vegetables.

One morning I found that our dog's neck was swollen Jinna looked at Dadoria and said "He must have been bitten by a cobra."

"Will he die?".

"No, he'd have died before his neck became this size if it was a bad dose."

Dadoria had become a great hunter. He pounced on snakes, however dangerous they were, and Jinna had a hard time saving a rat snake he had pinned down. He went for anything; a mongoose, a hare or a bandicoot had only to appear and Dadoria would be after it into the jungle.

We were resting in the cave one day after putting in a spell of hard work on a *maniocca* plot.

"Your father must be looking for you everywhere," said Jinna.

"I'm sure he hasn't been able to get news of us. Perhaps he thinks we've gone out of the country."

"Or that we've gone up to Colombo."

"Siripala must be at school yet. Ranadeva was to go to work in a shop in the hill country. I wonder if he did."

"Did you tell them we were running away?"

61

"No. There wasn't time for that."

"The police must have been looking for us."

"I don't think so. I think that story was made up just to scare us."

"If we got to the *copra Mudalali's* we might get news of the village."

"Let's wait a bit longer. We could take a trip a few months from now. We can collect the money by selling *maniocca* and *batala*."

The soil of the island was very good and our *batala* flourished. We took *batala, vatakolu, pathola* and *bandakka* across the river to the village. After six months the *maniocca* was ready. From that time on we had to cross the river every week to sell what we grew.

We spent very little on food and clothes and next to nothing on hired labour, just a few cents for porterage into the village sometimes. We were able to save steadily and had put by two hundred rupees by the end of our first year.

We cleaned more land on our side of the island and our *hena* became quite a plantation of *batala, maniocca* and vegetables. When the rain came we planted twenty coconut seedling and fifteen plantain runners in the flat land below the *hena*.

Podi Gamarala often visited us and praised our work. He slept with us in the cave sometimes. "What sinfulness!" he said whenever he saw me fishing.

One night Jinna saw the floating fire again. We had forgotten all about it. Our excitement came back. What was the secret of that moving light? Perhaps it had appeared many times since, though we hadn't been looking out for it.

We ran along our jungle path but soon had to give up trying to press on, for the jungle was too thick beyond the place where we had stopped work. We came back and kept a lookout from the high rock we climbed the last time, too.

We saw the strange canoe again. It was making for the other side of the island.

"Jinna! We haven't done anything about this! The last time, too, we saw the boat soon after the light. There's some big mystery here."

"We should have explored the other side long ago! We could have gone round in the boat one afternoon."

"What's the use of going there by day? The light appears at night. So does that boat."

"But if we go there by day we might still find some clue….."

"We must go now."

"Through the jungle? How can we?"

"No, not through the jungle. We must take the canoe." I said impatiently.

"The boat will be smashed to pieces on the rocks."

"We must row far out beyond the island and then make for the other side."

"That will take five or six hours, at least!"

"I think we can make it in three or four. The boat should be going back to the other side about dawn."

"It's sure to be gone before we get to the other side. And who knows where we'll end up going ashore in the dark? Let's wait for daylight."

I was used to doing as I pleased. I picked up an oar and went down the path to the landing-stage, saying "Oh well, if you're afraid…."

Jinna caught up with me before I could get to the pier.

"I'm with you, whatever happens to us. Let's go… he threw his oar into the boat and pushed off.

We made upstream, steering for a point on the river bank. There was a stiff land breeze against us. I hadn't thought it would be so difficult.

"What did I say! Jinna was panting heavily as he pulled on his oar.

The canoe rocked in the waves set up by the breeze, the spray hissed against its side. We were moving very slowly. The fishermen were keeping close under the banks. The trees were all bent one way by the wind, their tops swept back, like a crowd running into the wind. The spray flung up by the oars blew into our faces as if propelled by some machine. The breeze was gaining force every minute, churning up the water frighteningly.

I was so tired that I had shipped my oar for a while but I threw myself into the work once again trying desperately to keep the boat going upstream.

"Don't let up," said Jinna redoubling his efforts. "If we don't keep at it we are sure to be dashed to pieces on the rocks."

It took us three hours to work round to the other side of the island. We were then able to head for the creek.

"Oy!" shouted a fisherman who was paddling towards the far bank of the river. "Where do you think you are going? Don't take your boat in there! It's all rock…. You'll be dashed to pieces in this wind!"

"What did I say?" said Jinna.

"Keep paddling!" I said. The danger made me more determined. I was full of excitement at the chance of an adventure after months of working on the *hena*.

The fisherman's boat was close to the other bank now and moving fast under its sails so we couldn't hear what the man was shouting. We were still making for the shore of the island when we saw a boat emerging from a gap in the rocks.

"There! That must be the boat! Faster!" I said.

"Faster! I'm so tired I can't row at all."

We were both so tired that we could scarcely lift the oars. The other boat was pulling away from us. We shouted, but then Jinna said that they wouldn't hear because we were shouting into the wind. It seemed to me that the rower was a woman. I realized I was right when Jinna too pointed it out. There was another figure in the boat, a boy who was sitting in the middle.

What made the woman row to this deserted island in the middle of the night? What was the light we had seen? Why was the woman stealing away before daybreak?

After resting awhile we tried again to get   inshore. This side of the island was protected like a fortress by masses of rock. We came three or four times to the point from which the other boat had appeared without being able to find the passage. Over and over again  we touched submerged rocks while threatening outcrops of granite jutted out of the water on every side.

"Let's turn back," Jinna shouted angrily.

"All right! But I'm coming back tomorrow. I'm going to track down that devil even if it takes all day. And I don't care who he is!"

Jinna was  now as eager as I was to unravel the secret of the island.

We turned back.

"We didn't even bring a gun," said Jinna. He was even more daring than I when he scented real danger.

"Yes, we didn't think of that."

"We must bring one tomorrow. We don't know what we'll find here. We mustn't come just swinging our hands."

We had to struggle for half an hour to get to midstream again. From there on we had the wind behind us and the boat gathered way. We only had to steer it towards our landing place.

## CHAPTER VIII

## A STRANGE GUEST

Jinna was up early next morning. He cooked rice, *sambala* and dried fish. We rarely had rice in the mornings, so I asked him why.

"Aren't you going after that *mala yaka* today? If you aren't, I'll go alone!"

Jinna gave me an enormous helping of rice.

"There! Eat to fill your stomach!"

"But is it good to eat so much in the morning?"

"Once we start looking for that devil today I don't know when we'll get back. We must keep on at it even if we have to do without eating rice till evening."

Jinna ate two platefuls of rice, washed and put away the plates and then began to collect the things we would need to take with us. He went into the cave for the two big knives.

Suddenly, he ran out of the cave screaming" Mother! I'm finished!" and fell on the ground. I lifted him up to our stone platform and looked back into the cave. It was a cobra! It's head was as large as a *kenda* leaf and it had raised itself about a foot and a half above the ground. It was swaying about and going "Hoa!hoa!" But I wasn't frightened, I was very angry, I ran into the cave for the gun and took aim at the top of the cobra's hood.

"Apoi! Don't shoot!" shrieked Jinna, clutching at me and pulling me down. I lost by balance and went down with Jinna. I turned on him angrily though he was writhing in pain. "Don't! Don't shoot him!" he shouted.

"Who?"

"The cobra!"

He looked ghastly. He was making a great effort not to cry out. I remembered reading in a newspaper that plantain juice was an antidote to cobra poison. But I couldn't go for some with the cobra still hissing in the cave.

"I have to kill it! I must go for some medicine, idiot!"

"Don't kill! *Nai Hamy* won't bite me again. Run for the medicine.

"*Nai Hamy*!"

"Don't talk like that about cobras......Go for the medicine – please. I can't bear it any more" he said twisting about in pain.

I picked up the hatchet and a cup and ran to the waterside. I cut down an ash plantain stem, sliced it up and squeezed the pieces to get a cup of juice. Jinna drank it up.

"Where's the cobra?"

Dadoria came running out of the jungle and went into the cave. "You come now, you!" I said, aiming a blow at him.

He ran toward the landing stage. Jinna smiled when he saw how angry I was.

"*Nai Hamy* glided away slowly."

"And where do you think his highness has gone now?"

"Oh, just somewhere I saw him gliding away."

"Well, if you want to get bitten again, go ahead! I'm not taking any risks!" I searched the grass near the cave and the undergrowth. When I cam back Jinna was looking much better.

"I'll ask Podi Gamarala and get a *vedarala*," I suggested.

"Wait a bit, the pain is less now. I think *Nai Hamy* really hit the handle of the knife. I just got a scratch."

I looked at his hand. He was right. The only injury was a little scratch on the back of his hand.

"If just one of the fangs had struck true I'd have been finished," he said.

"How" you know so much more about cobras than I do?"

He smiled painfully. He must have thought I was praising him  for  he began to tell me all about it.

"I have heard a lot about them. My uncle was a snake-bite *veda* and my father, too, has treated people who had been bitten."

"Then you must be knowing all the cures."

"No, I don't know any. My uncle never taught us what to use."

"You might feel worse later. I'll  go and see Podi Gamarala."

"Don't. wait a little longer, You can go in a while if you really need to."

"The cobra must have gone into the cave in search of frogs. He's sure to get in again. And you didn't want me to kill him!"

"It's very wrong to kill a cobra. They take revenge, in fact they remember a wrong for generations. Besides, this cobra was a female – they are the worst...."

"That's exactly why we should finish it off!"

"Don't say that - once a whole family was destroyed because a cobra was killed."

"But we don't have families, man! And now its sure to want revenge – don't forget I tried to kill it."

"No – that was a she cobra. A she cobra goes   to a place because of love."

"Love?" I laughed. "She must have bitten you out of love, then!"

"I didn't mean love for me."

"Who, then" I can't understand your *andara demala*. Can't you stop speaking in riddles?"

"She must have come because she loves you."

"Me?"

"Yes!"

"Why should she love me? I'm not a cobra!"

"Don't say that," he said putting on a *Mahadenamutta* look. "That must be your mother. She has come back because she loves you so much. She must have bitten me because she is angry with me for bringing you here. It was only a warning – that's why she only scratched me. She could have bitten my hand quite easily."

I was very upset by Jinna's story. I know that grown-ups believed such things, that the dead could be born again as cobras because they wanted to protect their own. But I had never thought about it seriously. I hadn't thought about the possibility this time either. Mother born again as a cobra – mother, who had loved me more than her own eyes – the idea filled me with hopeless anger.

"You say my mother is a cobra and has come to see me? I said angrily.

"I can't exactly, but it must be your mother because she followed you out of the cave when you went for the juice."

"Then I tried to shoot my mother?"

"Yes, I think so."

"Don't give me any more of that buffalo talk?"

"It's not buffalo talk, *mahattaya*! It's true. They say these things in the sacred books!"

"Mother, a cobra! If you dare say that again I'll break your teeth!" I threatened.

I hardly knew why I was so angry. But I felt a terrible hopelessness at the thought of such a thing happening to a wonderful woman like mother. She had been so good to everybody, not only to me. And I had tried to shoot her. I think that was why I was so angry.

"Don't be angry. Upali *mahattaya*. I'm only telling you what's written in sacred books."

"When have you read sacred books?"

"Well, I have heard people who read those books talk about it My father and mother used to tell such stories."

"But who is this man who reads sacred books?"

"Grandfather Kiri-appu"

"Grandfather Kiri-appu! That old idiot's lies would split granite! So you learnt scripture from that gypsy?"

"He knows a lot of scripture."

"Look, don't tell me about him Jinna, don't say I didn't warn you. I'll knock the teeth out of your jaws with this gun butt if you tell such stories about mother again!"

70

Jinna didn't say another word. But I was very upset for a long time. I was still very young, after all, and the thought of mother becoming a cobra because she loved me so much kept coming back disturbingly for months afterwards. I wasn't angry with Jinna any more, but the thought itself was too much for me. For a long time after, the mere sight of a cobra made me feel a strange mixture of anger and childish fear.

I gave Jinna another cup of plantain juice and ordered him to get some sleep in the cave. Then I put two of my fishing rods into the boat and pushed off into mid-stream. You had to get out into deep water to catch fish like *parati*, *katilla* or *kalanda*.

I baited the hook and cast one line, fixing the rod to the boat. Then I tried with the other line too. There were other fishermen some distance away. They were doing very well, pulling two or three fish every minute. They were using horse-hair lines and small hooks and were going for small *katilla*. I was using gut lines and large hooks and expected to catch bigger fish, like *parati* and *kalanda*.

There was a jerk at the end of the line that bent my rod from the rip to the handle. I thought I'd got at least a big *paratiya* and I drew the line in carefully. It wasn't a *paratiya* but a large *petthaya*. It's a beautiful fish with black and yellow stripes, but fishermen detest it. I threw it back into the water. It pulled itself up like a whitish balloon and floated upside down for a while before righting itself and swimming away.

Just then my other rod jerked and almost touched the water. When I caught it up it bent over like a bow. The fish began to swim away strongly under water as if it was trying to break the line. I played it for a while and pulled it in slowly. After about a quarter of an hour the fish was so tired that I was able to bring it alongside and lift it into the boat. It was a big *paratiya*.

I think fishermen have more than one reason for liking a catch of *parati* more than anything else. *Parati* are strong swimmers who put up a good fight, they look elegant with their neat shape and colour, they fetch good prices.

Next came another *petthaya*. I was quite angry as I threw it away and watched it float downstream.

I took home a catch of two fine *parati* and two sizable *ranna*. Jinna was better now but still too weak to do anything but lie on the rock. I made him a rice porridge and cooked myself a fish curry to eat with my rice along with some *maniocca*.

In the afternoon I went to the *hena*. I weeded the plot where the young *maniocca* was coming up and cut down three bunches of plantain. I pulled out the soft inner layers of the stems and threw the rest into the river. In the evening I ferried the plantains and some vegetables to the village, taking the *kesel-bada*, too along as a present for Podi Gamarala. He was, I knew very fond of *kesel-bada* curry. I got good prices for the vegetables and plantains and was able to buy everything we needed.

It was quite dark when I got back. Jinna was sitting on a rock near the landing stage waiting for me.

"Are you all right now?" I asked.

"Much better, but I feel very weak."

"You'll be all right if you have some rice for dinner."

Jinna took a week to return to normal and join me at the *hena*. Then we found that the *maniocca* was ready for harvesting. The soil was so parched that it was very difficult to dig out the *maniocca* and we had to use pickaxes to break up the hard earth. But we managed to pull up nearly four hundred weights of *maniocca* and about three of *batala*. Some of the yams were as large as a man's shank. We took it all across the river, but this time the prices were rather low.

The rainy seasons were coming. We burned down more jungle and dug up the ground for a new *hena*. We planted it with *maniocca* and *batala*.

With all this to be done, we had no time to explore the other side of the island.

Our island was becoming famous. The villagers were impressed by the loads we carried across the river and they even began to look out for "*Madol Doova batala*" and "*Madol Doova vegetables*."

Other villagers besides Podi Gamarala began to visit us. Even parties of visitors from Colombo who had come down for fishing sometimes came across. We often made them have a meal with us. They seemed very glad to know us and everybody praised our farming. Some of them asked us to visit them in Colombo.

Among the others were a lawyer from Galle and his family. Podi Gamarala brought them over. We gave them a meal of rice, *maniocca*, coconut *sambala* and dried *kumbala*. The lawyer's wife praised our cooking and said that the dessert of *kirala* fruits with syrup was excellent.

"We haven't had better food even at home," said her husband.

You boys must come to our house in Galle," said the wife."

Their little daughter plainly thought we were heroes and asked us innumerable questions about the island. She said that she and her brother would spend the next holiday on the island with us.

"Come, we will be very happy," I said. "But if you have to eat our food for a week you won't want to stay on!"

"No, no. We like your food very much. We would never stand for eating rice and *maniocca* and *pol-sambala* and dried fish at home, but here it was marvelous!"

"We could go boating every day with Giniwella." said her brother, who was a little older than she.

They listened round-eyed to the story of Jinna and the cobra and laughed heartily when I told them that Jinna believed that the cobra was my mother.

"How did you make sure, Jinapala?" said the girl.

"Sure, little sister" Whenever a cobra, particularly a young one, is seen in a garden people always say that it must be fond of the people of the house."

The mystery of the floating light and the woman in the boat made them quite determined to come again.

"We really must come here next holidays." said the girl. "You are not to explore the other side without us. *Ayya* will bring father's gun with him, we'd better have two guns."

I gave the children bags of *cadju* and *kirala* fruit., and their mother half a sack of *maniocca*. The lawyer wanted to give us twenty rupees but I wouldn't have it. So his wife gave us a nice comb, two cakes of soap, a towel and a tin of biscuits.

"We expected to use them here. We don't need those things any more. We're going back tomorrow. There's plenty at home! But I'm sure you boys could do with some."

I tried to take just a cake of soap. Then she left the other things in the cave. The children gave us two English books.

"But I don't know English."

"It doesn't matter, keep them to remember us by!" said the girl.

"We'll teach you English during the holidays," said her brother.

"I've gone up to Grade Two," I said.

"Oh! Then you can go on learning very fast. We'll send you some books – some that will be easy to understand. You'll know a lot more by the time we come back."

All the next week we were hard at work on the *hena*. We did some weeding and planted more *maniocca* and plantain. Our plantain orchard was so large now that we were able to take some to market two or three times a week.

"We must go after that *mala yaka* soon," said Jinna one day. "Shall we go tomorrow?"

I agreed.

But there was so much to do on the *hena* that it was ten o'clock before we were ready. We had to work on the *batala* beds every morning besides seeing to the young plantain and coconut plants.

We were about to start when Podi Gamarala came to the island with the headman and another government official. They wanted to hold an inquiry because we were farming the island without permission. But the man from the *kachcheri* felt sorry for us when he saw the *hena* and our plantation of coconuts and plantains.

"This was a thick jungle when we came here," I said. "No one ever came here. You couldn't go ten feet from the waterside because of the thick undergrowth. We had to fight the jungle and we have worked like slaves for two years to grow all this."

Podi Gamarala took our part.

"*Aney*, the boys have worked very hard, they are very clever lads."

"I can see that," said the official. "The trouble is this, you can't cultivate government land without a permit. You have broken the law. I am supposed to take you to courts."

"*Apoi!* Will we have to go away, then?" I asked sadly.

"If anyone else wants to take out a lease you'll have to go."

"Please we'll pay a rent.....You must give it to us somehow."

75

"Plenty of people are willing to pay good money to lease this land." said the headman.

"Oh, everybody wants the island now!" said Podi Gamarala pointedly. He turned to the official.

"Pardon me, sir, but the headman is behind this. These boys have worked very hard. They take good loads of *batala* and *maniocca* to the shops across the river. And look how big their plantain cultivation is. Our headman has now told people in the village that they could get hold of all this if they leased the land. Those people are now waiting for a chance to grab all this and drive these boys away."

"Government won't take the land away from the boys to give it to anyone else. But if people want the land, they will bid for it, and then these boys will have to bid higher."

"Please sir, give it to these boys. They have worked so hard to grow all this," Podi Gamarala pleaded.

"I'll do what I can. But it will be difficult if other people want to bid. I can see that the place really belongs to the boys, but you know what government regulations are Podi Gamarala, we cannot go outside the law."

"We'll bid – we don't care how much.: I said.

"Quite right!" said Podi Gamarala. "Let them all bid! We won't give up, If you don't have enough money I will lend you whatever you want."

The official told us to come to the Galle *Kachcheri* the next day. We gave them a drink of *Kurumba* from one of the coconut trees and pressed the *Kachcheri* official to take some ash plantains with him. He wouldn't accept the gift.

"Take them sir." said Podi Gamarala, hoisting the clusters of plantain to his shoulder. "They are honest straightforward boys. They are not trying to bribe you. They just like you, that's all. Do whatever you think is right. You are only doing your duty. Let the people who want the island go ahead and bid for it. I know how to take care of them and their plantation!" he said threateningly.

"More than half the produce goes to Podi Gamarala," the headman whispered to the official.

"That's a lie Sir!" I said. I was furious that such a thing should be said of the one man who had helped us. "Podi Gamarala helps us a lot. He always has."

When I told Podi Gamarala why I had flared up he smiled out of the corner of his mouth and his eyes flashed like live embers. He could turn quite nastly when provoked.

"Let his honour the headman say what he likes. Why should we care" he said coolly.

The headman knew what Podi Gamarala could be like if he lost his temper. He bowed his head and walked away.

I went to Galle with Podi Gamarala next morning. We first went to the friendly lawyer. He and his wife welcomed us warmly. The lawyer went with us to the *Kachcheri* and spoke on our behalf to the official and even to the Government Agent. There were many other applicants but the Government Agent agreed to give us the lease at twenty five rupees a year. I paid up for the two years that had already passed and for the next year, too.

We spent the afternoon at the lawyer's house. The children came back from school and made me eat all kinds of sweets. They took me to the Fort, and we walked along the old ramparts. They showed me the lighthouse, a big hotel, the esplanade and the courts.

"Father's cases are mostly in the District Court," said the little girl, showing me an ancient building. Then, pointing to some huge *Suriya* trees. People wait there under those trees until their cases are called."

We went to their house. I wanted to go to the Railway station.

"Stay here today, Giniwella," said the girl. "You can go back tomorrow."

"Jinapala is alone on the island. I must get back tonight."

"Why didn't you bring him too?"

"There wouldn't have been anybody to look after the *hena*."

The children gave me two English books. "They are very easy to read. One is a story about Robin Hood. You are sure to like it."

"You must come to *Madol Doova* next holidays."

"Oh yes, we're coming. *Aiya* would love to go fishing in the river."

When we were ready to leave the boy stretched out his hand. I wasn't used to this and put out my left hand.

The girl laughed. "Give him your right hand, Ginwella."

She caught hold of my right hand and gave it to her brother. "When we were leaving the island that day you shook hands the right way. The day in town has upset you!"

Podi Gamarala laughed. "He's not a boy to be upset because he doesn't know English ways. He's a tough young fellow!"

The boy squeezed my hand warmly and his sister too, did the same with a beaming smile.

"It's easy to learn English ways. We'll bring spoons and forks with us when we come to *Madol Doova*. We must teach you how to use them!"

"Then he'll want to wear trousers, too!" laughed Podi Gamarala.

"Why not? He could do that, too!"

"He'll have to give up farming then!"

"Why should he? He could wear shorts. It will make the work easier."

We left Galle rather late in the evening and reached *Madol Doova* just as dawn was breaking.

## CHAPTER IX

# THE FLOATING FLAME

Jinna was wildly happy at the news. "We must tell everybody at home that we have a big plantation now! Let's go back to the village for a week or so."

Jinna's suggestion made me, too, think of home. What did father feel about me now? He must have searched for me everywhere. What did my stepmother think of me after my disappearance? Her son could not be more than ten now. They would be delighted to hear that we were doing so well. Could Dangadasa be still at school? Had Siripala left the village?

"We can't go just now?" I said. "We must work hard and farm the whole island. Let's wait a little longer before going back.

"Ranadeva must have left school by now," said Jinna. "Dangadasa must have gone upcountry to work in a shop. His father wanted him to become a trader."

"They must have forgotten us by now. I heard in Galle that the teacher from Dickwella is now at the Devature school. We must go and see him the next time we go to Galle."

"Wasn't he the one you stayed with at Welikanda?"

"Well, the Welikanda headmaster did go to Dickwella, but I can't be sure that this is the same person. There must be many teachers at the Dickwella school. It's a big school. I would like to see Mr.Dharmasingha's children again."

"If he hears about you he'll write to your father."

"I won't tell him where we are if I met him. I'll say that we have got work upcountry."

We heard Dadoria bark suddenly near the cave. We ran to the cave. Dadoria was jumping about before a python that had caught a hare. Only the hare's legs could be seen. Dadoria became more violent when he saw that we were with him. I picked up a pole to attack the snake but Jinna jumped forward and stopped me.

"What's the matter? Will the python too, try to take revenge? I laughed.

"No, a python is not like a cobra. But you shouldn't attack an animal when it is eating. It's a great sin," said Jinna taking away the pole.

"I didn't want to kill the python, I only wanted to save the hare."

"There's nothing left of the hare to save. It's already two thirds dead!"

"No, look, it's still alive. It will live if we get it away.

"Live? Not when a python has been at it. An animal hasn't a chance even if you pull it out. The part that's inside must be pulp already." Jinna caught Dadoria round the neck and dragged him away to the cave.

I could see the python's gullet swelling steadily. I saw the hare's body going down to the snake's stomach and even heard a faint sound of bones being crushed. I went back to the cave.

We set off to explore the other side of the island next morning. Jinna took the hatchet and a big knife while I took the gun and the biscuits given us by the lawyer's wife.

No breeze, not a leaf stirring. The smooth expanse of water gleamed jewel-blue in the morning sun. The boats and fishermen by the distant rocks were mere silhouettes. The water had a beautiful silver shimmer where it caught the sun. The going was made difficult by a continuous carpet of water weed. Bits of the weed came up with the oars, and at every stroke dozens of shrimps leaped back into the water from the weed like a shower of puffed rice.

When we finally got through the floating water weed to the deep water it was much easier to steer the boat as we wanted. We pulled out for about three hours and then changed course to the right. We soon found ourselves struggling with the weeds again. The going became slower and slower, and then the boat stuck fast as if we had stuck a sandbank. We were so tired that we just shipped our oars and sat there panting.

"What a journey! My joints are just lifeless. It's like rowing the boat on dry land! If there's a rock somewhere under these weeds it might hole the boat."

"We're not going back today without going ashore there somehow," I said. "If anything is going to happen to the boat, let it! We could swim to a rock."

"It takes the life out of you. I don't think anyone has taken a boat through here for years. That's why this has got so thick."

We tried again after a good rest. The boat moved like a turtle stranded on land. After about an hour we managed to get clear of the waterweeds only to come up against a threatening wall of rock.

We steered back and forth but couldn't find an opening anywhere. We had been rowing about for nearly half an hour before we found a tiny channel between huge masses of rock. Trees and creepers made a thick roof of foliage over the channel making it a gloomy cavern between the rocks.

This had to be the way taken by the strange boat. We went through into the shallows and ran aground near a *kirala* tree. When we got out of the boat we sank to the knees in mud. I took the gun and the biscuits with me and Jinna followed with the hatchet and the knife.

We broke through the thick growth of *karan* bushes to come upon a faint path through the jungle. We couldn't tell whether it was a game track or whether it was man made.

"The woman and the child from that boat must be using this path." Said Jinna.

We followed the path for some distance and came upon a large open space in the middle of the jungle. A large slab of rock on one side and a miniature mountain peak on another showed why no trees grew there. There must be solid rock under the thin topsoil. Even shrubs and bushes hadn't taken root here.

There seemed to be a log lying on a rock to the right. We approached it cautiously.

"Crocodile!" shouted Jinna.

It was basking in the sun and lay as if dead though we were quite near it.

"Is it dead?"

"Don't go any closer!" Jinna shouted. "That's what they do when they come ashore. They play dead."

"Shall I take a shot at it? Lifting the gun to my shoulder.

"Don't!" He shouted again. "That *mala yaka* will hide if we give ourselves away like that."

I threw a piece of rock at the crocodile. It jumped off the rock and we heard it crashing through the undergrowth and into the water.

We crossed the open space and came upon another track through the jungle. It led us to a glade beyond which lay a little hill. We could see the opening of a cave among the rocks. Just then we heard someone clearing his throat. I was reminded at once of the sound I heard the first time I set foot on *Madol Doova*.

I peered through the bushes and there he was! A man was squatting on the ground. A thick beard covered his face. I could just see the eyes, nose and forehead. I was so startled that I called out "Jinna!" involuntarily. He must have heard me for he stood up and stared into the bushes.

I threw myself on the ground and cocked the gun. Jinna threw himself down beside me with the hatchet in his right hand. I don't know what made us crawl up on the man. The fear I had felt at first had vanished. Jinna's foot slipped, and a stone crashed into the thicket. The man jumped up and rushed into the cave. He came out with a gun and peered into theundergrowth. We had barely taken cover behind a large rock when there was a deafening gunshot. We saw the man run back into the cave through the smoke.

"Why did he run back into the cave? I asked Jinna.

"His gun must be a muzzle-loader. That's why there was all that noise and smoke. He has run into recharge it! Quick! We must get that gun away from him even if we have to kill him, or we'll be done for!"

We rushed out of the bushes and looked into the cave. He was a big man and yes, he was pushing the ramrod down the muzzle of his gun. I fired into the air, reloaded, and covered him.

"Don't move! Stop, or I"ll shot!" I cried fiercely.

"Careful! This is a breech-loader !" I heard Jinna say.

"Pull down that gun! I yelled.

He stared at us as if he had turned to stone. The gun fell from his hands to the ground.

I kept him covered while Jinna went into pick up the gun.

"Another minute and he would have finished us off!" said Jinna.

"Are you taking me away? said the man. He slipped down to the ground and covered his face with his hands.

"Take you away? Where? What for? I said.

He looked up fiercely.

"Aren't you gentlemen from the police?'

"We aren't gentlemen, man; we are from the other side of this island. From the *hena*....."

"We thought there was a devil here!" said Jinna. "That's why we fought our way here somehow."

The man had got over his scare now. He spoke very humbly, as if he was our servant. He had heard only a few months ago that two people were growing vegetables on the other side of *Madol Doova*. Before that his wife had come across the river once a week. They had made it about once a month when they heard about us.

"It was the light bobbing up and down that made us come here," I said.

"That was me, I wanted to scare people away."

He showed me a thick pad of coconut fibre and cloth and an open earthen ware *hattiya* full of coconut shell charcoal.

"I pour *Kekune* oil on the cinders. It blazes up like a torch."

"Oh! So that was the floating flame!"

"Your *gini hatti pooja* made us come here!" said Jinna. "If we hadn't seen it we wouldn't have known that there was anyone here. We wanted to hunt down the man or *mala yaka* or whatever it was only after we saw the flame and the boat."

"What do you eat?"

"I cook here. I've grown some *maniocca* and *batala* behind the cave. Every two or three weeks my woman use to bring me rice, coconuts and the *lunu miris* for curry. She only comes after two or three months now."

"We have seen two people in the boat."

"She brings our son with her. They bring me everything I need. The rocks keep fishermen away from this side of the island. People don't dare come anywhere near the island after dark."

"Why?"

"They think it's haunted. And they believe there are cobras and vipers everywhere."

"The ghost stories must have started because of your *gini hattiya*!"

"No. There have been terrible stories about *Madol Doova* from before anyone can remember. In the old days fishermen who had drifted near the island at night sometimes saw such awful things that they became ill. Some of them died later. I came here because I had nowhere to go.

"Have you never gone home since?"

"I have. Every three or four months or so. On full moon nights."

"What? It will be easier to recognize you when there's a moon."

"No. It's safer then. No one goes fishing on Poya nights. There's nobody on the water. And people go to the temple at night. I don't stay beyond about two o'clock in the morning. My woman rows me back. She's even better with the oars than I am. She's a good swimmer, too,"

I thought her a heroine. I would have liked very much to meet her.

"We must come one day when your *hamine* is coming." I said. I felt it would be wrong to say "Your woman" when she was so clever and daring.

"I'll ask her about it the next time she comes" he said. We shared our biscuits with him.

It was very difficult to get him to tell us why he had come to *Madol Doova*. He was obviously afraid that we would give him away. In the end, when it was nearly time for us to go back to the *hena* I decided to try a threat.

"If you don't trust us, how can we trust you? We have to look after ourselves. We will have to tell the police about you."

"Well......But will you promise not to tell anyone else?"

"No," we said in unison.

He told us the story at last. He had killed a man. He was part-owner of a piece of land. He had worked hard on it and made it a very fine *hena*. When the *maniocca*, *batala*, and plantains were giving him a good yield two of the other owners claimed a share. They didn't even live in that part of the country. He had driven them away. A fortnight later one of them had come back with some rowdies and cut down the plantains and pulled out the *maniocca*. Balappu couldn't stand it any more. He had threatened them with a hatchet. The rowdies had set upon him in a bunch and he had fought back. He had injured two of them and split open the head of a third. The man had fallen dead and the others had run away.

"My woman wasn't at home that day." He said If she was at home the other three, too, would not have escaped alive. She's worse than I when she's really angry. She could take on two men single handed. She came running home as soon as she got the news. When she saw what had happened she told me at once to go Colombo, take a ticket to India, throw it away somewhere and then find my way here to hide."

"So you got to Colombo before the police caught you."

"Yes, and I bought a ticket to India the next day. I even told people at the station where I was going. I got off the train at Ragama and walked all the way back to Dehiwala. I took a train from there to Godathara. Then I walked to Kahanda. It took days. When I got there I waited till nightfall and then took a boat that was moored by the bank. I rowed it here. Then I stripped, left my shirt on a rock and folded my sarong into a loin cloth, I got into the boat again, rowed it out into midstream and then swam back. The boat went downstream. I don't know where. I knew that people brought noosed snakes to the other side of the island so I came ashore on this side and made my way through the jungle."

"Through the jungle!" I said in amazement. "We tried to get through for day! It was impossible."

"It wasn't. But I had to get to safety somehow." It took me three days. I lived on cadju, mangoes, himbotu, wild dates and such things. When I got through at last I found this cave. I lit a fire that night as a signal."

"How did you make a fire?"

"It took me half the day. I had to rub two sticks together for hours. My woman came over the next night. With rice and some cooking pots and boxes of matches. Things were easier after that."

"Didn't people begin to ask questions when they saw your *hamine* row out here every two or three weeks?"

"No, she began to take a boat on the water nearly twelve years ago. She used to ferry people sometimes. People call her the *Kakulukari* because she sells crabs."

"Does she go after crabs alone? Do you catch them with a net?" I asked.

"She is very clever at it. She goes out alone. You don't catch crabs with a big net. You have to use small hand nets baited with fish. You have to put down twenty or thirty nets at various places along the river and then go back when it's daylight. The nets are like bags and the crabs are inside eating the fish. Not everyone can do it though. If they catch a finger, between their pincers you can't get it away easily, they almost cut it in two. First you have to catch them by their legs very quickly. Then you have to grip the pincer arms firmly and fix them shut by sticking a small wooden peg behind the joints."

"How do you remember where you put down the nets?"

"You let them down with a string. You fix a float to each string to mark the place."

"You must make a track through the jungle to our side." I told Balappu.

"I won't need to make a path. I know how to get through. But it's not at all easy, it takes three or four hours."

We went exploring in the jungle behind the cave. The jungle was even thicker here than it was beyond our *hena*. *Katukurundu* trees and *Eraminiya* bushes grew everywhere. *Mee* and *Kekuna* trees, too, seemed to be common here. Where there were no thorn trees were anthills in which snakes might lurk. Jinna discovered some wild dates and gave me some of the ripe red fruits. We made our way very slowly, picking a tortuous path through trees. We seemed to be in the depth of the jungle when we came across a small cave. We had to crawl on our knees and elbows to get in. A hare that had been sitting on a heap of white sand jumped right over my shoulders as we were crawling in.. There was a lot of this white sand and, sitting right in the middle of it, there was a human skeleton! It gave us quite a shock to come upon it like that, but soon curiosity and amazement overcame our fear.

The skeleton was stretched out on the sand. It hadn't decayed much. We wondered why the thumbs had been tied together, for although the string had decayed the position of the thumb joints clearly showed this. The toes, too, were placed against each other in the same way. On the ground, on either side of the skull, were two one cent coins. They were old Portuguese coins of the kind we used to call "blind" coins. The last decayed bits of a sarong lay near. The skeleton looked as if it had been laid out for burial. I noticed that none of the bones were broken.

When I came out of the cave I began to wonder about Balappu. Had he told us the whole truth? Could this be the skeleton of someone he had murdered? That story he told us could all be an invention. Why were those two coins there beside the skull? Who had put them there? Why had the thumbs and toes been tied together like that?

Alarmed and full of suspicion we went back to Balappu's cave. I had shouldered my gun but now I held it ready.

When we got to the cave Balappu was lying inside. He sat up. His face and eyes were trustful, entirely without suspicion. Should I talk to him about the skeleton. I wondered. I put it off. I was sure he had seen it. Why hadn't he told us about it? Had he thought that we wouldn't come across it?

"Did you got far into the forest, sir?" He asked me.

"Yes."

"There's a small cave there, did you go into it?"

"Yes."

"I didn't think you'd go in there."

"Why?"

"You have to go down on your knees to get in."

"Yes, we crawled in. There was a skeleton there on a mound of sand." I said, looking him straight in the eyes.

"I forgot to tell you about that."

Was he telling us the truth? Or had he kept silent because he hadn't thought we would discover the cave"

"How did it get there? Who could have killed that man?"

Balappu laughed.

"I don't think he was murdered, he must have died there."

"How do you know?" I asked  putting down my gun. I had been holding it ready all that time.

"This island was the home of a gang of robbers long ago at the time the English conquered this country. They waylaid travelers near Mirihi Kanda on the Galle Matara road. Whenever they heard that the police were after them they hid here. They must have lived here for seven or eight months at a stretch sometimes."

"Yes, I've heard stories from old people in the village about them – how they used to lasso travellers near Mirihi Kanda and haul them up to rob them."

"That's it – I have heard the stories too."

"Could it be the skeleton of a man whom they had murdered?"

"I don't think so." Said Balappu. "Did you look at it closely? You can see that the  thumbs and toes have been tied together. That must have been done after  that man had died. Did you see the "blind" coins on either side of the head?"

"Yes, how did they get there?'

"One of the robbers must have died here.  It isn't easy to dig a grave in this hard earth. They probably didn't have *udellas*. They must have buried their comrade in the cave and gone away."

"Why were the coins on either side of the skull?"

"They must have fallen off the head later. If you don't close a man's eyes as soon as he dies they remain open. People put coins on the eye lids to keep them shut because the staring eyes of a dead man can bring bad luck."

"And the coins have fallen on either side of the head!" I understand now."

"Yes. I think that is how it happened. Everybody around here  knows about the robbers. The villagers can  tell many stories about them."

"I remember now. Podi Gamarala did tell us about them once."

"Podi Gamarala? Who's that?" He asked in alarm.

"He owns the *hena* on the other shore."

"I've heard of him. He knows many government officials. Please don't tell him about me."

"No, we won't. But he's a very good man. Well couldn't this still be someone who had been killed by robbers? Perhaps they quarreled among themselves and one was killed. They could have hidden the body in there."

"I don't think that is what happened." Said  Balappu. "There's no sign of an injury anywhere. He must have died of some illness. If he had been killed there should be some sign, like a broken skull."

"How did that mound of white sand get there?" I asked.

"I can't make it out either, I haven't seen that sort of sand anywhere on the island."

"There was white sand under the wild date trees by the stream," said Jinna. "But this sand looked whiter than that to me."

My doubts about the skeleton disappeared.

"Not a word about me  to anyone, please," Blappu pleaded again.

"Don't be afraid, Balappu, we won't tell anyone. A man from the Kachcheri came to see us a few days ago. People had sent petitions against us. The headman was trying to give our *hena* to somebody else. That official told the Government Agent all about us. The Government gave us the lease and we have already paid the money. No one else will come here now."

"Yes, and I don't think people will ever come to this side of the island. Anyone coming to the island is bound to come ashore on your side."

"We won't talk about you to anybody. If we hear that anyone is likely to come round to this side we'll tell you about it somehow. But we would like to meet your *hamine.*"

Balappu laughed.

"I'll ask her one day. You can even go to our house. She will enjoy that. She likes boys of your sort."

We got back home very late in the evening.

"So the *mala yaka* has become a man!" said Jinna. "If we don't tell the government will it be wrong?"

"I don't know really. And we can't ask Podi Gamarala for advice."

"Why can't we?"

"Didn't you hear? We promised not to say anything to Podi Gamarala."

"Oh, let's just leave it at that. How could we know anything about a man on the other side of the island? We'll say we've never been there."

I laughed.

"How can we say that if Balappu decides to visit us here?

"Let's tell him not to come."

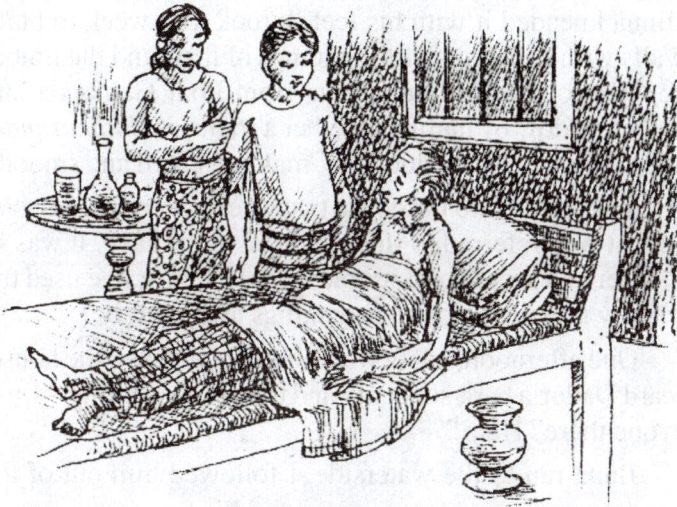

# CHAPTER X

# THE RETURN OF THE PRODIGAL

We began building a house not far from the cave. Podi Gamarala showed us how to level the ground and plan the house. He decided where the door should be and the window and how the single room should lie. He insisted that even a small house had to be built according to some old rules that he knew by heart as otherwise we could have bad luck. He recited some verses and explained their meaning to us. In the end we had to give up our own ideas and do as he wished.

Podi Gamarala marked out the room and the verandah on the ground, by stretching cords between pegs fixed in the ground. The plan was exactly that of one of the old fashioned little houses you can see everywhere.

We felled some trees and put up a timber frame to which we fixed the roof. We thatched the roof with straw. Then we cut down two large *Kenda* trees and split them up. We made a framework of *Kenda* scantlings and laths of bamboo. It was like the skeleton of a house. We quarried clay from the hillside and Jinna kneaded it with his feet. It took us a week to build the walls with the clay by fitting lumps of it around the timber frame. We got an old door frame from Podi Gamarala and made the window by nailing together a frame of *Katukurundu*. We used the clay for the floor, too, making it hard and smooth.

We moved into the house two weeks later. But we soon found that we preferred to sleep and rest in the cave. It was so much nicer and more comfortable than the house. We used the house only as a place for storing things away safely.

One afternoon, a few week after we finished the house, we heard Dadoria bark suddenly and then a man yelling "*Apoi*! Is anyone there? Help!"

Jinna ran to the waterside. I followed him out of the cave.

Jinna was already coming back, dragging Dadoria along by the neck. Behind him came a young man who looked like a beggar. His sarong was old and tattered and his shirt was filthy. His hair had not been cut for a long time and was all tangled up. He tried to smile at me but it looked more like a grimace of pain and he was panting heavily. He came up to the cave, looked around cautiously and flung himself down near the entrance.

"Haven't had even a drop of water today." He whined. "I am very hungry.....so weak, I can hardly talk......"

Jinna looked from him to me and laughed.

"Do you think this is your own home?" We cooked only enough rice for ourselves."

"Please give me something, too."

"Where have you come from?"

"From Palossa, But my home is in Wellaboda."

"What's your name?" I asked sitting near him.

"Punchi *Mahattaya*."

"Punchi *Mahattaya*! And your father and mother?"

"Pappa and mamma are both dead."

"Punchi *Mahattaya*." "Pappa and mamma" he seemed to be from a well-to-do family. I began to feel sorry for him. Jinna still looked suspicious but I told him to give the stranger some rice and *maniocca*. We watched in amazement as he gobbled down three platefuls of rice with *pol sambala* and dried fish.

"He seems to have starved for days." I whispered to Jinna.

"He's no Punchi *Mahattaya* when it comes to eating." Jinna said it out loud for Punchi *Mahattaya* to hear. "Doesn't like the *maniocca* I think."

Punchi *Mahattaya* had a drink of water and then went to sleep. He fell into a deep sleep, snoring loudly. Jinna and I finished eating and went back to the *hena* to harvest some *maniocca* and *batala*.

Upali *mahattya*, that fellow is no punchi *mahattaya*. He's a fraud." said Jinna, after he had pulled up a few yams.

"I don't think he's a fraud. He looks slow and lazy but that may be because he has not had food for a long time."

"No I am sure he's a rogue. We must watch him."

"You don't like him, do you?"

"No, it's not that he's not taking anything that is mine. But it's the truth. I'm sure. He's shady. Where have you put the money, *mahattaya*? Don't leave anything out. Lock it all up. He might pick up whatever he can and run away."

"The money is in the inner room and I have the key. How can he get away from here?"

"Why, our boat? If he takes that….." Jinna picked up a large centipede with a stick and threw it away. It had been hiding under a *maniocca* plant.

"I don't think he's that sort."

"But it's better to be on the lookout."

# MADOL DOOVA

I got Punchi *Mahattaya's* story from him little by little.
I think it showed that he was not a thief but an idler who had
got into trouble. Jinna, of course didn't believe the story at all.

His father had been a landowner....people had called
him *Hamu Mahattaya*....and his grandfather had even been a
*Mudaliyar*. Punchi *Mahattaya's* parents had loved him dearly
but his father had died when he was ten and his mother when
was fifteen. He had then lived with relatives for ten years.
They had found him a nuisance, for he did nothing and had
finally turned him out. He was too lazy to work and had become
a *thakkadiya*, living on his wits.

I asked him how he had come to the island.

"After pappa and mamma died I lived at uncle's house.
After sometime aunty tried to make me do the work that
servants do." He said 'aunty' and 'uncle' as rich people who
know English usually do. "They wouldn't have done that if
pappa and mamma were still living. In those days I wasn't
even allowed to play on the street. I refused and went to stay
with my mother's sister. But they too began to scold me and
say nasty things about people who lived on others. I went from
one relative to another after that, staying a few days at each
place. Sometimes I went to faraway towns and got money from
people by using pappa's name and telling them that I was
stranded. Everybody pitied me when they saw what I had come
to. But some people said sneering, that people who call their
father pappa deserve what they get."

"How can you believe all that?" Jinna whispered.

"Listen, will you."

That was how Punchi *Mahattaya* had gradually become
a vagabond. He told us of the incident that had made him
come to *Madol Doova*. This was after he had been going from
one relative to another for some time. When their sneers
became too much for him to bear he had gone back to the
village.

96

There was a miserly old woman there who was very feeble and almost blind. Fifteen years earlier her son had gone to look for work in Colombo and had never come back.

Punchi *Mahattaya* had got hold of a cloth and coat and even a pair of shoes, and had gone to the old woman's house when her servant was out.

"Mother!" he had called, disguising his voice.

"*Aney*, who's that?"

"Why, mother can't you recognize your own son?"

"My son? My son who went to Colombo?"

"Yes mother. Here I am. After fifteen years. When I was all alone there in Colombo I often thought about you, and how you had always been so good to me. Tears came to my eyes whenever I remembered you."

The old woman had come right up to him and touched him. She had felt his head and hands and stroked his fingers and had even smelt him.

"You have changed so much! You were not like this when you went away."

"I changed a lot after going to Colombo."

"Sit down, sit down." She said, kissing his hand with tears of joy.

"Sit down! I've come to stay, mother! It's time I looked after you, isn't it?"

"It was so good of you to think of me, son! I am blind now. I can't go anywhere. Thieves come every night for our coconuts. Now they are stealing them even in the daytime."

"I'll give them coconuts, now! Wait and see," he said. Then he went close to her. " I must run mother.....No time to sit here talking. All my things are at the station. The box of crockery, the two beds, the armchair, the wardrobe, my clothes, and the bag of rice…everything I brought I have to pay more than I expected at the station. I'm short of fifteen rupees. Give me fifteen rupees, I'll hurry across to the station and bring everything here in a bullock cart."

"How can I find so much money, son?"

"Quick, search in your big *pettagma* and collect fifteen rupees somehow. The things at the station are worth at least eight hundred rupees."

The old woman hobbled away into the house and took nearly a quarter of an hour to come back with three five rupee notes. She took his hand and put the money in it, saying, "That's all I had...."

"That's all I had......."

Punchi *Mahattaya* got away with the fifteen rupees. When the old woman's relatives had started searching for him he had escaped by going from one village to another. That was how he had reached the island.

"Didn't I tell you he was a thief?" said Jinna triumphantly.

"But he isn't. Would a proper thief have told us such a story about himself? He is a terrible idler, certainly. He'll do nothing as long as he has something to eat. And when that's finished he takes what he can from people."

Punchi *Mahattaya* stayed on with us. About a month later, Jinna said he had had enough.

"I can't let him, carry on like this any more. He's just eating up everything without doing a stroke of work. I asked him to bring us a pot of water from the pond the other day and he refused without a second thought. He has heard you call me Jinna and he has started doing it, too, Upali *Mahattaya*. When I told him not to do it he snubbed me. He said that his pappa was a *Hamu* and asked me what my father was."

"People from feudal families are like that" I said trying to make a joke of it.

"Family! If he tries it on me again, I'll starve him!"

"He'll be better when he gets used to this life. He'll help us with the work."

Punchi *Mahattaya* was the greatest shirker I have ever seen. If I managed to get him to the *hena* he turned the earth over once or twice with the *udella* and then sat down on the nearest rock panting as if he were ill. "What a sin!" he could say if he saw a worm or a beetle that had been injured when we were digging. Jinna was so irritated that he emptied a basket of decayed leaves over his head. He merely cursed Jinna and went off to sit on another rock. "I must go away in a day or two," became his reply when Jinna wanted something done.

"Why don't you? What are you waiting for?" Jinna shouted at him."

He slept late into the morning, getting up long after Jinna and I had returned from washing ourselves. Once Jinna poured a pot of water over him, soaking him from head to foot. I had to lend him a sarong until his own tattered cloth dried out. He ate more heartily than ever and when he finished he asked Jinna to give him a cup of water.

"I'll give you water! It's all I am here for!" said Jinna, glaring at him.

Their quarrels became annoying. I laughed at them when I could, but it came to a point where I had enough.

"Ey, Punchi *Mahattaya*!" I threatened him. "You don't do anything here except eat! That's why you are so quarrelsome. Get up and come to the *hena* with me. We have some digging to do."

I picked up an *udella* and gave him another. He tried the same old trick of turning over a few clods of earth and stopping to rest. I shouted at him and made him go on. I did this over all day, so that he really had to do some work. Of course he grumbled all the time. He didn't stop grumbling even when we went back to the cave to eat.

After three months of this Punchi *Mahattaya* put on a little weight and began to look much better. He worked harder now. Sheer idling must have thinned his blood and made him unfit for work when he first came to us.

One evening the lawyer from Galle came to *Madol Doova* with Podi Gamarala. He took a sheet of the Sunday *Silumina* out of his pocket and gave it to me.

" I turned out here to give you some news."

"News?"

"Look at the advertisement on page four just above the editorial."

The headline was Upali Giniwelle, I read eagerly;

"Upali Giniwelle

Your father is seriously ill and his life is in danger. He often calls out your name and is anxious to see you. Please come home at once. He has a heart disease and cannot be cured. Forgive us if we have wronged you in any way. Your father and I await your return eagerly.

Your Stepmother

I read this over three times and then thanked the lawyer.

"So your mother is dead?" He said.

"Yes, she died when I was very young."

"Did you leave home without telling your father?"

"Yes."

"Your stepmother must have treated you badly."

"No, I wanted adventure, so I left home with Jinna."

"My son and daughter, too, felt very sad when they read this. They asked me to tell you that they had not forgotten you. They want to come here next month when they get their holidays."

"Please send them here. We are expecting them."

"But you will have to go home to see your father, Ginwelle. You shouldn't refuse to do that."

100

"Yes, yes, I'm going to see him. But I won't stay more than a week or two. I'll be back soon."

We gave them roasted cadjunut with kitul candy. Podi Gamarala had coffee with a piece of candy.

"Who's this new young man?" said the lawyer looking at Punchi Mahattaya.

"Punchi *Mahattaya*. He's from a good family."

"Punchi *Mahattaya*? Where is your home?"

"Wellaboda."

"Where is Wellaboda?"

"Near *Mudaliyar* Dunuweera's"

"And your father's name?"

"He was called Lata Dunuweera *Hamu*."

"Oh! Then you are *Mudaliyar* Dunuweera's grandson?"

"Yes…"

The lawyer didn't ask any more questions. He knew all about Punchi *Mahattaya* and his family, he told me as we went down to the waterside. Punchi *Mahattaya's* father had made no effort to earn a living and had squandered everything the Mudaliyar had left. He had died suddenly. My friend had not known Punchi *Mahattaya* before but had heard about him. He knew the story of how the old woman had been cheated.

"When will you go?" Podi Gamarala asked me as he got into his boat with the lawyer.

"Tomorrow."

"That's good, don't delay."

When I was ready to leave next morning, Jinna's eyes were full of tears. Punchi *Mahattaya* too looked very sad on my account. He was really good-hearted, I thought to myself, though he was certainly lazy and had been up to so much mischief.

101

"I won't stay away more than a week, Jinna." I said. "You two must look after everything well."

"I would like to see your father, too, Upali *Mahattaya,*" said Jinna.

"Why, yes, you can go as soon as I come back."

"But I can't go alone!"

"Well, we could go together then. Punchi *Mahattaya* can look after the *hena* till we come back!"

They rowed me across and I walked all the way to Talpe station. I took the evening train to Matara and got to Kamburupitiya at daybreak.

Father was very ill. The tears gushed from his eyes when he saw me.

"I feel very ill, ; I won't live much longer."

I thought I would break down.

"I will go to Galle tomorrow morning. I must get you a good doctor," I said.

"We got down a doctor from Matara, He's treating father now, " said my stepmother.

"But we can get a specialist from Galle, too," I said.

"Yes, putha, that will be good" She said. She went towards the door, and I saw that she had something to tell me. I was following her when father called me to him.

"*Aney, putha*, it's good you have come. I don't feel so bad now. I thought I would never see you again. Your stepmother thought of putting that notice in the paper."

"A lawyer from Galle brought me the paper."

"Yes, how lucky that was! *putha*, I won't recover. I get an attack every three or four days. I don't think I will live through the next one. The doctor has already told them that..."

"I'm going to fetch you another doctor from Galle."

"No need, *putha*...I know this is not an illness that can be cured. Don't waste your money.... You must look after your stepmother and her son. They have nothing. The shop did not bring in anything during the last two years. I had to borrow money. When my debts are paid there will be nothing left….. There's no one else to support them. Are you earning anything now?"

"Yes, father. And I don't mind giving them everything I earn. Jinna and I started a *hena* and it brings in a fair amount. We have nothing to spend it on there. We save quite a lot."

I went out of the room to meet my stepmother. She was crying. As soon as she saw me she came over to me and kissed me on the forehead.

"I came away from father's room because I thought I would start crying there. It is so good that you have come. We must do everything to save him. We can sell all these things….."

"We don't have to sell anything. I have a little money with me. I don't need it. I'll do everything I can for father and give you any money that is left over."

She was still crying. I think she felt that she was to blame for my going away from home.

"Forgive me, *putha*, " she said, tearfully, looking away. "Forgive me if I have done wrong. I didn't wrong you knowingly. But I must have hurt you when I lost my temper those days…"

"No, *kudamma*. I didn't run away because I was angry with you or father. We just wanted adventure. We did it in fun."

"*Aney, putha*, I have felt terrible ever since father fell ill. I couldn't help thinking that you left home because I had hurt you. I haven't slept at all these nights. Father wanted me to go to bed, but I sat up there until I fell asleep where I was. After an hour or so I would wake up again."

She was a pretty buxom woman when I left home, and now her flesh barely covered her bones and she looked a skeleton.

"Don't stay up any more. I'll sit up by father."

"*Aney putha*, it is not lack of sleep that has made me so thin, my brain was on fire with father like that and then I began to think about you...."

I went to Galle the next day and managed to get the Chief Physician from the hospital to come with me. He examined father carefully. He told us that the doctor from Matara could go on treating father. A heart condition like that couldn't be cured, he told me.

Father died a week later. We gave him a good funeral. Seven days after the funeral we had the memorial almsgiving. We gave alms to twelve bhikkus.

A day or two later I went to Matara and bought forty yards of white linen and some clothes for *kudamma* and my stepbrother. I also gave her what money I had left keeping back twenty rupees for my return to *Madol Doova*.

"What am I to do with all this money, *putha*? I can manage on whatever we get from our property here. But do something for your brother... that's all I ask of you. Couldn't you live here with us now? Now that father is gone I want to look after the two of you. It will be a comfort to have something to do."

"Don't worry, *kudamma*. I will send you the money for *malli's* education"

I looked for my old friends. Ranadeva was the only one left in the village. Siripala was an apprentice in his uncle's shop in Batticaloa. Dangadasa was a clerk in a shop in Agrapatana. Ranadeva and the headman's son were always up to some mischief in the village.

But they helped me a lot with the funeral. They and their friends made the grave, they cut down arecanut trees for the thorana by the graveside, they stung up the lines of young coconut leaf to decorate the route. I wanted them to take thirty rupees to treat all the helpers but they wouldn't touch a cent.

"You seem to be rich now, Upali" said Ranadava.

"Well, we don't lose money anyway."

"We'd like to come there for a week or two," said Hinni *Mahattaya*.

"Come, We would like that very much."

"What do you grow there?"

"*Maniocca, batala*, bananas, vegetables… that sort of thing."

"You wouldn't have been able to do all that if you hadn't Jinna," said Ranadeva.

"Of course. I could never have managed alone. I wouldn't have dreamt of going to *Madol Doova* without Jinna."

"If you'd stayed behind you could have been one of us!"

"Just as well. You would have become a loafer, too. There's nothing to do here," said Hinni *Mahattaya*.

"But it's better than living on a desert island!" said Ranadeva, laughing and throwing an arm around my shoulders. "You're the only one we miss, Upali."

"Why do you say that? Siripala and Dangadasa have gone away, too."

"They weren't of much use. But if you were here we could have faced up to anything! Did you know that Lalitha is married to a trader upcountry?"

"Yes, I heard, " I said smiling.

"Before she married she was always asking me about you. I told her that no one knew where you had gone."

"She would be glad to see you, Upali!" said Hinni *Mahattaya*.

"That was before she got married! She wouldn't want to see you now." Said Ranadeva, looking at me with a laugh.

It was time for me to go back. Ranadeva spent the last two days at our house. He gave me all the village news, all that had happened since I left home and particularly stories of what he and his friends had said and done. The cadju story had gone no further, " Go and tell the police," the headman had said when Upasakkapu complained to him. Upasakappu had replied that the headman was saying this because Ranadeva and Siripala were his nephews.

"Well, is this a thing to file action about? That these children took some of your cadju? Just tell their parents about it, Upasakappu!"

Ranadeva told me that father had searched for me everywhere, from Hambantota to Colombo. When he couldn't get a lead anywhere he had started writing to traders he knew in various places. He had even got a friend to write to someone in Singapore.

"Uasakappu doesn't talk to me yet. "Ranadeva said, next morning when we were having a cup of tea before leaving.

"Really."

"Yes, that man is vicious. I could get all his cadju trees chopped down now if I wanted to."

"Don't. We were in the wrong after all."

My stepmother wept again when I set off. "Forgive me if I have wronged you." She cried.

"You haven't *kudamma*. If anyone did wrong, it was I. I gave you and father endless trouble."

She kissed me on the forehead again. I patted my stepbrother on the head before leaving for the station with Hinni *Mahattaya* and Ranadeva.

"I might come to your place if I feel like it," said Ranadeva.

"Please do!"

"It will be to stay! If I come, it will be because I'm sick of this village."

"Good! We could cultivate the whole island then."

"He'll never leave here for good!" said Hinni *Mahattaya*.

"But I really might think of going away."

"Thinking alone won't do!" I said.

I saw them waving to me long after the train had left the platform.

It was late that night when I reached Podi Gamarala's house. I stayed the night with him and crossed to *Madol Doova* in the morning.

Jinna was very sad at the news of father's death. Punchi *Mahattaya,* I was glad to see, was a changed man, He was no longer pale and   sickly and he was as brisk as Jinna now. He ran off to get a pot of water from the pond.

"Was he very nasty to you? I took the chance to ask Jinna.

"He tried to be, once or twice. I told him off, and threatened to beat him. That settled him. He began to do some work. After a bit he changed suddenly. He seemed to put on flesh visibly. He does a lot of work now."

"I'm sure it was all a matter of food! He was half starved and couldn't do anything properly and this gradually made him lazy. He started boasting about his family as a cover for his laziness. When people talk about the status of their parents they are usually trying to avoid doing some honest work. Do you think he will stay on?'

"He'll stay… we are good friends now. He made all those new vegetable beds  over there."

"Did he? He likes the work now. We must start clearing another part of the island."

"Soon after you left, an Inspector and a policeman came here."

"What  for?"

"They had heard that a murderer was hiding on the island. We said we hadn't seen anyone else here. Podi Gamarala told them the same thing. We used to see a ghost some nights," he said. But that too, has vanished after these boys came here. The policemen searched the jungle behind the cave and the *hena* and went away."

"Did you tell Podi Gamarala that Balappu was living in a cave on the other side?'

"No, I didn't tell him anything."

"Does Punchi *Mahattaya* know?"

"No, I didn't tell him either."

"The policemen might come again. I wonder if Balappu has gone away. We haven't seen his wife rowing across for a long time."

"Let's go over there again," Jinna suggested.

"Not so soon. Let's leave it for a few months."

Punchi *Mahattaya* came back with the pot of water. He put it down and came over to join us.

"Jinna says you're very good now," I said, smiling at him. "We must start work on another part of the island. We'll give you a share of whatever we get."

"I don't want money." He said. "What would I do with it? I'll stay as long as you and Jinna are here."

"That's good!"

I put an arm round each of them and we went down to our landing stage. Doadoria was following us, when we heard a *korawakka's* call, and dashed off into the bushes. We sat on the rock under the shade of the *kirala* trees.

The scent of ripe *kirala* fruits masked the smell of leaves dacaying in stagnant water. The breeze came over the water glittering in the sun, and with it a touch of warmth that was very pleasant to both body and spirit. Some of the fishermen on the water were already rowing back to the bank, many were still fishing, their boats dotting the surface of the lake. One boat seemed to be heading for the island, there was a man standing in it, his right arm bent to make a throw with the net that hung from his fingers. On the other side the forest stretched from beyond. Podi Gamarala's *hena* far way to the horizon. A great stillness hung over the big forest, the far hills and the calm, blue expanse of water, merging into the endless silence of the sky. A strange pang of sadness went through me as I took in those immense silence. Father dead, my stepmother old before her time, repining over the past and facing a future of bleak loneliness, my old friends, all scattered, I would see those friends but rarely, if indeed, I was ever to see them again.

" I must go home again soon. Jinna." I said as my unaccustomed sadness grew deeper.

"I'm coming too."

"Yes.. yes; we can make the journey together this time. Punchi *Mahattaya* will look after everything here till we get back."

I turned to Punchi *Mahattaya*.

"We want to go home for a few days. Are you afraid to stay here alone?"

Punchi *Mahattaya* turned back to look at the cave and the jungle beyond.

"No," he said, and a smile touched the corners of his mouth. "No, I'm not afraid of anybody. Not of the night, not of the jungle or the animals. I'm not afraid of anything. And there is nothing I want."

I am fearless too, for my nerves are quite strong. Punchi *Mahattaya* was, I think fearless because of a great indifference. He was always cool, and misfortune could not trouble him.

---

**THE END**

109

# GLOSSARY

| | |
|---|---|
| Ambalama | An abandoned house used as a resting place. Originally meant a roadside resting place for t ravellers. |
| Katti | A game played between two teams. |
| Kidaram | A bushy plant about 2 feet high. The flowers give an offensive odour. |
| Almariya | Wardrobe |
| Mudalali | A prosperous entrepreneur. |
| Kaththa | A heavy iron hatchet. |
| Eramudu | A tree with a thorny bark. |
| Mala Illawwa | Devil take it. |
| Kalli; pandu | Games played by children. |
| Veddhas | Aboriginal inhabitants of Ceylon. |
| Kos | A tree with large flat oval leaves each about the size of the palm. |
| Iratu | The thin stiff central rib of the coconut leaf. |
| Opisara Hamine | The wife of the headman. |
| Apoi amme | Literally "Mother help me", Heaven help me." |
| Galibba | 'Tough (like a hard-shelled tortoise). |
| Halapa | A sweet pancake made of millet flour. |
| Hatti | Shallow earthen cooking pot. |
| Porisadaya | Vandal (literally cannibal). |
| Menna bung | Look man. |
| Kuna | Miser |
| Hantenna | Destination (in this instance, the balaya fishing ground) |
| Ingura | A veriety of small red fish |
| Balaya | A variety of small red fish. |
| Kelawalla | A variety of large blood-fish (species of Tuna). |
| Maniocca | Tapioca. |
| Pol sambala | A preparation consisting of scraped coconut, chillie, onion and dried blood fish. |
| Samba | Small grained variety of rice. |
| Ambul thial | A preparation of fish in a black sauce. |

| | |
|---|---|
| Kachcheri Mudaliyar | A minor titular appointment. |
| Gadol manuma | A game. A one cent coin is tossed on the tiled floor. The player whose coin is closest to the centre of a square tile takes all the other coins. |
| Karavala | Fish salted and dried in the sun. |
| Na and la | Sinhala equivalent of the sounds of na and la. |
| Colomba-rala | Colombo fellow. |
| Kokilaya | A tuneful bird. |
| Magadi Natakaya | Mock play. |
| Magadiya | Trickery. |
| Baniama | A loose jacket open at the top. |
| Copra | Dried kernel of coconut used for extracting oil. |
| Hena | Cultivated plot of virgin land. |
| Batala | Sweet Potato. |
| Doova | Island |
| Kadol | A species of mangrove. |
| Kirala | A swamp tree with a sweet smelling edible fruit. |
| Udella | Mammoty. |
| Udekki | Small drum. |
| Veena | Violin. |
| Mala yaka | Deadly devil. |
| Nai hamy | An endearing way of addressing a cobra. Lady Cobra, literally. |
| Vedarala | A practitioner of traditional medical therapy. |
| Andara demala | Meaningless babbling. |
| Mahadenamutta | A folk story, character epitomizing foolish pontification. |
| Mahttaya | Sinhala equivalent of 'Mister' |
| Aiya | Elder brother. |
| Hamine | Madam |
| Keselbada | The tender core of the trunk of a plantain tree. |
| Thakkadiya | Rascal. |
| Pettagama | A wooden box. |
| Hamu | 'Mister' |
| Putha | Son. |
| Kudamma | Stepmother. |
| Bhikkus | Buddhist monks. |
| Malli | Younger brother. |
| Thorana | Pandol. |
| Korawakka | A Water hen. |

111

# Author

Martin Wickramasinghe was born on the 29th of May in the year 1890. in the Southern village of Koggala. It was in these beautiful surroundings, bounded on one side by the reef-fringed sea, and on the other by the broad sweep of the Koggala Oya, one of the largest fresh water lakes in Sri Lanka, that Martin Wickramasinghe grew up. The landscape, the flora and fauna, the forested hinterland, the lake and the sea, and the changing patterns of the way of life of the people of the village were the background that Martin Wickramasinghe later immortalized in his novels and short stories.

Martin Wickramasinghe applied modern knowledge in literature, linguistics, the arts, philosophy, Buddhism and comparative religion, education, and natural and social sciences to discover the enduring roots of our national identity that exists in our folk life and culture. It was largely through his work that the modern Sinhala novel and short story came to maturity. Madol Doova, the trilogy consisting of Gamperaliya, Kali-Yugaya and Yuganthaya, Viragaya and Bava Thranaya are amongst his best known novels. Bava Tharanaya is a novel inspired by the life and times of Prince Siduhath Gauthama.

## Translator

Ashley Halpe was Professor of English in the University of Sri Lanka. His poems in English have appeared in Commonwealth *Poems of Today*, *Young Commonwealth Poets* and *Adam International Review*. Other than *Madol Doova*, he has translated Martin Wickramasinghe's short stories *Vahallu*, (Slaves) and *Leli* (Daughter-in-law). These have appeared in *Adam International Review* and in *PEN Asian anthology* respectively.

# MARTIN WICKRAMASINGE BOOKS IN ENGLISH

## ASPECTS OF SINHALESE CULTURE

An extremely valuable collection of essays on certain aspects of sinhalese culture undergoing change due the influence of other cultures.

## BUDDHIST JATAKA STORIES AND THE RUSSIAN NOVEL

The study of the Jataka Stories in relation to the stories of Dostoevsky, Gorky and Chekhov will provide literary and psychological insights for a penetrationg study on life and revel in his experience

## MADOL DOOVA

Madol Doova, a story of youthful vitality in the enchanting background of a southern Sri Lankan village. Has sold over a million copies in nine languages.

## LAY BARE THE ROOTS

Martin Wickramasinghe's enviable faculty of evoking, sound and sensation impart an immediacy that makes the reader share and revel in his experience.

## REVOLUTION AND EVOLUTION

The author brings insights from Buddhism and Hinduism into an erudite discussion of the views of Albert Camus, Teilhard de Chardin and Darwin amongst others on psycho-social evolution and revolution.

## FROM THE CRADLE

Glimpses of Sri Lankan Folk Culture portrayed at the Martin Wickramasinghe Museum of Folk Culture

## BUDDHISM AND CULTURE

The author of the book concludes….." I am aware that my interpretation will be unpalatable to those Buddhist scholars who hold to the letter rather than to the spirit of the Buddha's teaching.

## THE MYSTICISM OF LAWRENCE

Revelation of Lawrence's Mysticism and his attitude to sex as an affinity to Indian Tantricism.